Mumze
Love,
Susan
Xmas 1999

CHILDREN OF THE MAKER

Also by Lucy Cullyford Babbitt

THE OVAL AMULET

CHILDREN
OF THE
MAKER

Lucy Cullyford Babbitt

Farrar, Straus and Giroux

New York

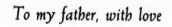

To my father, with love

O Essai!
Maker of all on earth and within,
You are wrong.

Your daughter Magramid, my sister,
Last-born and least deserving of your faith,
Is quietly destroying your good plan for life.
She has hold of just one colony, I know;
Yet even one gone wrong works to undermine the whole.
When it is in your power to stop her
So easily . . .

It is painful to admit a failure.
But even you, my Maker, must confess a flawed creation.
She is dangerous.
She is contrary to your plan of perfection for the mortal
    earth;
She is contrary to my plan.

O Essai . . .
Shouldn't you be at least as careful,
As caring,
As I?

—Jentessa

CHILDREN OF THE MAKER

1

It *was a windless night*, the air hung thick with ocean smells: the mustiness of algae-covered rocks, the stench of seaweed strewn along the shore—and the fish! The smell of fish hovered over the sand and crept into the village, calling all creatures of the dark to come and feast. But it was the cats who came in numbers to investigate the traps of water in the sand, claiming the carnage scattered on the beach.

The man came, too, hungrily down from the cave-home he shared with his mother above the sea, to find dinner. With an old net wound around his waist, he made his way gingerly through the swarm of cats, using both hands as a balance to keep from provoking their claws, until at last he reached the safety of the water and waded in. Knee-deep in the black sea, he peered down, his net poised for a catch. He could see nothing, but he could feel the things swimming invisibly by his legs. With a great splash, he plunged the net in and dragged it furiously back and forth—only to dredge up a weed.

He swore and plunged it in again, yet the fish kept eluding him, and when he saw some cats contentedly dining by the shore, he shouted in frustration and clambered out of the sea to rob them of their meal. The cats turned and hissed; the man faltered; then suddenly a queer sensation spread through his veins, and he lifted his eyes to the cave. Something was happening there. The night was so dark he could not tell what it was at first; but somehow the darkness seemed to be rearranging—thickening, almost—to a human-like shape.

The man forgot his hunger in an instant. He galloped across the sand, scattering cats, and scrambled through the tall grasses to the rocky facing. Feeling every step with the sure knowledge of his calloused feet, he was up to the cave by three rolls of the tide, and in it by the fourth.

"Mother!" he shouted, "you're here!" But he saw his mistake at once. It was that *other* one, the angry one, and he fell back in fright, knocking over a chair that had stood against the wall. He eyed the opening of the cave in desperate hope, but she was already moving toward him, blocking his escape, so he covered his head with his arms and whimpered, cowering on the ground.

But the Half-Divine was not thinking of the man. Jentessa's graceful hands reached out above him to a carving on the stone wall. The sacred symbol of the Maker Essai's plan—the Oval and the Rectangle entwined—was cut deeply and lovingly there from a time long ago when the cave had been a temple. Now the stone was crumbling, and Jentessa found a store of nuts tucked into the image for safe-keeping. Furious, she tore the nuts away, sending them flying through the air, then turned at last on the wild man.

"Where is your mother?" she demanded. "Where is Magramid?"

Another voice rose up behind her. "Here," it said.

The man cried out in relief, throwing himself at the older woman who stood by the entrance, caressing her skirts with his rough hands.

The two daughters of the Maker Essai faced each other then, in their mortal guise, their unnatural eyes unnaturally bright in that dim place; a moment later Magramid moved on into the cave, pushing aside her son indifferently.

"Why have you come, Jentessa?" she said. "We'll only argue; we can do that from the earth's Center." She went to a small wooden table and began picking through a pile of roots that lay there. "Did you net any fish?" she asked, turning to her son. He hung his head, and she turned away again, muttering under her breath.

"I have come to give you final warning," said Jentessa.

"Again?"

"This time I have the Maker behind me," said Jentessa, and when Magramid's eyebrow lifted, she added, "I *will* have It behind me. I promise you I will not rest until our circle of Half-Divines is purged of your mockery."

And then Magramid laughed: a soft, guttural laugh that echoed deeply in the cave. "Ah, Sister," she said, "when will you learn? The only creed our holy circle keeps is its hypocrisy."

"The Maker's plan is clear—" began Jentessa.

"But who wants to follow it?" said Magramid. "Why should we Half-Divines depend on the enlightenment of the Holy Intermediators to put our good thoughts and plans into play?"

"The Holy Intermediators are the proper human link between the Maker and Its people," said Jentessa.

"Proper, perhaps, but they're so rarely enlightened," said

5

Magramid, and smiled. "Why else would they continually choose such disappointing rulers in the Maker's name? You've had your share, Sister. It wasn't so long ago that your Melde Colony was completely in chaos due to some . . . inappropriate leaders."

"Every colony is due a crisis, Magramid," returned Jentessa sharply. "Don't try to change the matter of my mission. The point is, to what heinous lengths you have gone to violate the plan: You have told your people about all the other colonies; you are continually going in among your people in mortal form—and you make no attempt to hide from them that you are a Half-Divine; you interfere directly for your own twisted purposes."

"Even you have interfered, Jentessa!" said Magramid. "Don't you accuse me of the crime when you are fresh from it yourself."

"Only once have I interfered in all the Melde's history," said Jentessa, "and I never will again."

"Once is sin enough. You went among your people disguised in mortal form—as a Holy Intermediator, no less—to choose directly the present Rulers of the Melde. What gall. What nerve! What *violation*."

"At least I was disguised. No one suspected my half-divinity."

"Lies again! In the end, you told your Rulers who you really were. Violation number two. So don't come preaching to me about the sanctity of the Maker's plan, Jentessa. You're no better than I am—only more self-righteous."

Jentessa's eyes burned with fury, and around her the cave shook. The man, huddled again on the ground, pressed his arms tight around his head and wailed.

"There is no comparison!" said Jentessa. "I have made my colony great. It is perfect now. Even the Maker agrees."

"There *should* be a comparison!" Magramid shot back. "Why can you do whatever you want and be praised, while I would have to reinvent the stars to earn the slightest recognition? The smallest acceptance? I am damned whatever I do!"

"What you have done is ruin the faith of your people," said Jentessa. "The Vasser Colony lives in fear of you, without hope, without innocence. You even sinned—unforgivably with a mortal—and bore *that*." She pointed to the wild man. "How can the Maker praise you?"

Magramid's lips drew back, revealing her teeth. "At least," she whispered, "I have known passion."

"You will know the Maker's passion," said Jentessa, "because I will be watching you, waiting for the chance to show Essai once and for all what a damnable traitor you are to Its plan. I will be watching you . . ." With her glare still leveled on her sister, Jentessa's thickness trembled, then shrank into itself, fading out of mortal space, down into the Center.

The man's arms uncurled. He went to touch his mother's sleeve, when something in the fix of her shoulders warned him back.

Magramid stood still for some time; then she moved quickly, purposefully past the sacred carving, out of the cave and up the rough steps to the top of the cliff. The man followed her, uncertain, to where the rolling water spread itself long and wide below; where the quick, dark movements of the cats could just barely be seen. But when he joined her, he found his mother staring not out at the sea but in another direction entirely, back beyond the Vasser even, to the river.

His head dropped to one side with confusion; then with a twitch from his mother's arm, he knew.

"Don't go away!" he cried, clutching her.

"If one can go visiting," said Magramid, "then so can another."

"The Melde is an ugly place," he said; "don't go."

"How do you know if it's ugly?" snapped Magramid. "You've certainly never been there."

The man flinched at his mother's hardness, and sank back onto his haunches. "You said it had no sand," he answered, and then, with a defiant mumble, added, "You said it was ugly."

But Magramid was no longer listening. Her mind had turned again toward that distant river, and to that more distant settlement beyond.

"Oh, Sister," she said, her short white hair dancing in a sudden wind blown up from the sea, "you will know *my* passion." Her eyes shut tightly—and in the Melde Colony, where the water touched two rocky banks instead of sand, the river inexplicably clouded with mud, and tiny stones lurched up from the bottom. Notts, the Holy Intermediator of the colony, said it was an omen.

But no one in the Melde believed him. He was a good but rather silly man, who tended to overreact to things.

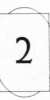

2

"*The two Rulers!* The guardians of the sacred Amulets," said Notts, "the Oval and the Rectangle, must never be apart." He hurried to fetch an arrow that had slipped from Paragrin's quiver. "Especially not in these troubled times."

" 'Troubled times?' " The Ruler Paragrin, the wearer of the Oval Amulet, took the arrow from the Holy Intermediator and led him, patiently, to look out the northern window of the chamber. Below them, the central court, bright with morning sun and cloudless sky, was the picture of normal activity. It was market day: furriers, weavers, and metalsmiths lined one side of the court with their wares; bakers, cheesemakers, and butchers lined the other; and a crowd of haggling customers joined the two from the middle. The healthy discord of a thousand conversations flooded the air, and away by the wide, flowing river, the song of a band of children could just barely be heard.

" 'Troubled times?' " said Paragrin again, and sensing that the little man was still not convinced, she pulled him gently toward the southern window, where the newly plowed fields of the Melde Colony lay rich and waiting beneath the spring-green mountain.

"I know, I know, I know," said Notts, shutting his eyes, "but the chosen two should always stay in the colony together . . . especially when there's been an omen!"

"Oh, that again . . ." Paragrin left Notts at the window and took up the rest of her gear: her hunting knife, her bow fashioned from the finest wood, and the bulging food-sack that her mate and fellow Ruler Cam—the wearer of the Rectangular Amulet—had prepared for her. "You made too much," she said to Cam, weighing the sack disapprovingly.

"Remember whom you're traveling with," he said, and Paragrin laughed.

"You're right," she said, and slung the sack across her shoulder. "Your brother Kerk will have eaten this by nightfall. Now, if there are no more dire warnings to be heard"— she leveled a look at Notts—"I'll head downstairs. Tell him there's nothing to worry about, will you, Cam? That I'll only be gone for a couple of weeks and that the silly mud in the water meant nothing." She rolled her eyes and strode from the room, the deer-pelt curtain swinging behind her.

Cam folded his arms across his chest. "There's nothing to worry about, Notts," he said. "She'll only be gone for a couple of weeks, and the mud in the water meant nothing."

"Why does she have to be so stubborn?" Notts lamented. "Not that I mean any disrespect," he added quickly. "I'm sure that trait served her well in the Battle last year, but these are different times."

"Peaceful times," said Cam.

"That's right," said Notts, then frowned. "Troubled times," he insisted. "They only *seem* peaceful."

"Come, my friend," said Cam, holding out his hand, "or we'll miss their leave-taking altogether."

"And why does she want to leave so quietly?" asked Notts, following him toward the worn steps that led down into the entrance hall. "I should at least be giving a public prayer for her safety before she goes."

"I wouldn't suggest it to Paragrin if I were you," said Cam.

At the bottom of the stairs where the mosaic stones of the entrance hall spread themselves out in innumerable patterns of Ovals and Rectangles intertwined, the rest of the well-wishers were gathered: just two young women, the only others privileged with knowledge of the quiet departure. The two stood comically close to one another, as if to show off to everyone the differences between them—Ellagette, the smaller, who was renowned for her beauty, and Atanelle, a large-boned, plain-faced woman who had single-handedly trained the forces last year for battle.

As Cam and Notts descended, Paragrin took Atanelle aside. "You know I'd much rather be going on this expedition with you instead of Kerk," she whispered, slipping an arm around the large woman's waist. "But you're our chief warrior, well, peacekeeper now, and I'd just feel better knowing you'll be here protecting, in case anything happens. If it wouldn't be too much trouble, I'd like you to keep a special watch on Cam . . . You know he doesn't always defend himself as he should."

"Oh! No trouble at all," said Atanelle, and her eyes shone. "I would have kept a special watch on him anyway, without you even asking."

Paragrin smiled. "I suspected you might."

"Just because he's a ruler, you understand," said Atanelle quickly, and blushed.

"Of course," said Paragrin.

"Where's Kerk?" Cam asked Ellagette when he had reached the bottom of the stairs.

"How should I know?" she replied, tossing her head. "Do you think your little brother tells me everything he does?"

Cam stared at her. "Have you two had another fight?"

"Certainly not," returned the other sharply. "Why do you ask?" and her mind went back to the exchange she had had with Kerk when he first told her of his plans.

"No, I'm happy you'll be leaving," she had lied. "It will be good for us to be apart for a while."

"That's just what I thought!" Kerk had exclaimed, and she had refused to talk to him for days.

Now Cam looked distrustfully at Ellagette's brooding expression, and turned instead to Paragrin. "Do you know where Kerk is?" he asked.

A look of annoyance began to spread across Paragrin's face; then she saw Kerk hovering with his gear in the dining room. "There he is," she said, and added under her breath, "It would have been just like him to be late. Anyway," she said, turning to the others, "I'll see you all again soon! Wish us luck."

"My Ruler! Won't you at least let me give a prayer here?" Notts entreated.

"No time, but thank you, Notts," said Paragrin, and motioning Cam to join her, she hurried out through the dining room toward the back entrance.

Kerk began to follow them, but paused, stealing a glance

at Ellagette. Her eyes met his, and for a moment the lovers held each other's gaze. There might have been some gentle words to say before they parted, but defiance still burned behind Kerk's eyes, so Ellagette dismissed him with an angry "Good luck, then," and left the Great House to go about her business. Kerk turned away from the embarrassed looks of Atanelle and Notts, and stalked out toward the back.

"Excuse me," he said when he pushed past Cam and Paragrin as they held each other by the door. "I'll wait outside. Take care of yourself, big brother!"

"I will," said Cam, and watched him go. "Trouble's afoot," he said to Paragrin. "They've been fighting again."

"They're always fighting," returned Paragrin, and pulled Cam closer. "I don't want to talk about them now. I want to talk about us."

"Why?" said Cam, stroking her hair. "*We* never fight."

"I've been a bear for months," said Paragrin. "It's just that you never fight back." She smiled, then looked down, playing with the lacing of his tunic. "I want you to understand why I need to go, that it has nothing to do with you."

"I do understand. At least you've tried to explain your reasons . . . the restlessness."

"It's more than restlessness. It's been welling up in me since last autumn—this anger. I'm tired of being Ruler, Cam. I miss being free of responsibilities."

"We've always had responsibilities," said Cam, "just different ones."

"Well, you did, maybe, having to look after Kerk, but I was completely free. Now, for one whole year," said Paragrin, "I've had the burdens of the whole colony on my shoulders."

"And you've carried them well," said Cam.

"Yes, I have. But I've started to resent it. Everyone who comes to me with a problem makes me angry these days. I know it's wrong, but I hate it. I feel as if I'm withering, as if I'm being stripped of my youth. It isn't fair, Cam! Other people have so much more freedom."

"Other people aren't rulers."

"Well, for two weeks, I'm not going to be a ruler, either," said Paragrin. "I'm sorry to leave you alone like this. The colony's burdens have been as much on your shoulders, I know they have, only somehow you don't seem to be bending under them."

"Oh, Paragrin, you're twice the leader I am—you're just tired," said Cam. "There's no reason—Notts aside—why you shouldn't have a holiday. You and Kerk both. And who knows? Maybe you will discover something useful along the river. Or maybe you'll just enjoy yourself. It doesn't matter."

"I wish you could come with me!" said Paragrin.

Cam laughed. "Now that *would* turn Notts's hair white. No. Besides, I'd rather stay here anyway. It'll be a challenge to rule alone, to see if I can do it."

"You can do it." Paragrin squeezed his hand. "Thank you. For everything."

She kissed him. His arms stole around her again and they held each other until Kerk called impatiently from outside. She released him and adjusted the bow across her shoulder.

"I love you," she said.

"I love you, too," said Cam. "Good journey." Paragrin nodded and disappeared through the back entrance. Cam watched the door swing shut, then turned away.

The hall of the Great House, empty now of people, was cold. The stones that made up the walls and foundation still held the winter's chill, and Cam shivered as he entered it. He hugged himself for warmth and glanced up at the intricate tapestries that hung against the wall, deciding for the first time that they were ugly. He needed more comfortable ground and climbed the ancient stone steps, back up to the bedchamber.

Just as he was about to push aside the deer-pelt curtain, a rustling sound from the other curtained room—used when the Rulers were siblings or some other unJoined relation—made him start. He paused, wondering why Notts or Atanelle would have wandered there; then he reached out and threw aside the drape.

"Help!" cried a voice. "Intruder!" and Cam stood accused and dumbfounded in the doorway, staring openmouthed at the occupant.

The old man who had been laying out his toiletries on the table had clutched his robe around him in horror at the sudden entry. When he recognized Cam, though, he relaxed, letting out a "Pooh!", and returned his attention to the table, choosing a polished wooden comb from among the implements. He guided it carefully through the thinning hairs behind his ears, making a gurgling noise in his throat that Cam knew could only be laughter.

"Oh, Grandfather . . ." he muttered.

"You shouldn't be so dismayed, my boy," said Ram brightly, admiring his hair in the looking-plate. "That ungrateful granddaughter of mine has gone now, hasn't she?" He looked back at Cam and smiled. "So! I've come home to take my rightful place again at last."

3

Paragrin and Kerk avoided the usual thorough-
fares altogether in their quest for a secret departure. Winding
their way through the forest that encircled the colony, they
walked until they were well beyond the riverside dwellings
to venture onto the bank. Once they were certain no one
could interfere with their escape, they burst from the woods
into the sunlight, and Paragrin danced for the sheer joy of
being free.

"I haven't seen you this jolly since before you were made
Ruler," Kerk declared.

"I know! So don't call me 'Ruler' anymore," said Paragrin,
stopping to catch her breath. "As long as I'm on this trip,
I'll be just as common as you are."

"I'm so flattered," said Kerk, "and believe me, I wouldn't
have it any other way. Now let's go! I want to get as far
as possible from this wretched colony before nightfall."

Paragrin danced one last time in celebration, kicking a
stone into the current of the river. An angry mushroom of
mud boiled up where it had sunk, and Paragrin laughed to
see it, when her nerves suddenly flared and she spun about
to find an old woman standing directly behind her.

"Who are you?" demanded Paragrin. "Where did you come from?"

The old woman said nothing, only stared at the Ruler with a fixed brightness in her ancient eyes, glancing from the Amulet to Paragrin and back again, questioning.

As Paragrin's nerves quieted, so did her voice. "It's just that you startled me," she said to the woman. "I might have fallen into the water."

"Let's go," said Kerk, tugging on her sleeve.

"Just a moment," said Paragrin, and waved him off. Kerk made a face and started walking away from them, slowly, just to make his point.

"You recognize me, of course," said Paragrin even more gently to the woman. "Don't worry, everything is fine. Cam will explain it all later today. I'll be back soon, I promise."

The old woman still seemed confused, so Paragrin put out a hand to comfort her, when all at once she broke from her trance and seized Paragrin by the arm, her sharp fingers digging into the skin like claws. Paragrin pulled back in alarm—in greater alarm when she realized she couldn't shake the woman off—then, without a word, the old woman let go, the imprint of her fingers still lingering on Paragrin's skin.

Paragrin backed away from her in horror, then turned and caught up with Kerk, swearing under her breath. "That's just the sort of thing I need to get away from," she muttered, and shoved the Oval Amulet beneath the lacings of her jacket, "having to deal with crazy people like that. Let's get away from here. Let's run!"

They were gone. Magramid watched them go, then moved her steps slowly, thoughtfully, toward the Melde.

*   *   *

As Paragrin left the confines of the city behind her, she began to feel young again—normal again—shedding her real skin in this gloriously unreal time. As free as Kerk now, she ran beside him. They were united, like the wings of one bird rediscovering flight, and they soared miles before the sun began to set and they landed together, breathless, on the riverbank. Kerk plunged his hot face into the current and Paragrin followed his example, letting the cold water trickle deliciously down her front when she sat up again.

Kerk fell back on the grass with a sigh. "So, friend," he said.

Friend! Paragrin liked the sound of that. Why had they spent so much time arguing in the Melde when they knew each other's souls so well?

"Yes, friend?" she answered.

"Is there any of the food that my brother prepared for us left?"

"You should know. Where is the sack? You claimed it last."

"You mean *that* was the rest of the food? I thought you were holding some back."

"Oh, Kerk! You finished it? I hardly got a bite," said Paragrin, "and I'm hungry."

"It's not a problem. Relax!" Kerk sat up, shaking the water from his hair. "I'll spear us a fish and you can cook it. Nothing's simpler." He leapt to his feet and began to look around for a proper stick.

"Actually," said Paragrin, rising, "I'd just as soon do the fishing."

"Both the fishing and the cooking?" he exclaimed. "No,

friend, I won't hear of it. I'm going to pull my share on this trip."

"No, I didn't mean that I would cook as well," she returned. "I meant, why don't I fish and *you* cook?"

He stared at her. Then he laughed and continued to sort through the dead branches at the forest's edge.

"Kerk," said Paragrin, starting to eye the sticks herself, "I'm not trying to be funny. If neither one of us likes to cook, we'll just have to alternate."

Suddenly the perfect spear was in view. She reached for it, but Kerk was as quick, and they snatched it together and stood there with the stick between them.

Kerk glared. Then, without easing his hold on the stick, he eased his expression. He laughed again and smiled at her, placing his free hand on her shoulder.

"Paragrin," he said, "I don't cook; I hunt. Remember that I was never trained to prepare food as you were. To this day, even though my brother feels at home in a bakehouse, I still consider the practice more fitting for a woman's smaller, more nimble hands. I'd only be clumsy."

His voice was soft, apologetic, his dark eyes filled with sincerity. Paragrin looked up at him. Why was she feeling so suspicious? He was her friend, wasn't he?

"Well . . ." she said, and he reached toward her, gently brushing aside a fallen curl.

He might have succeeded, might have won her over, if—at the same time as he was touching her hair—he hadn't pulled the stick from her loosened grasp. The motive for it all became too clear in that instant, and Paragrin seized the stick back with a vengeance that surprised him.

20

"Rot you, Kerk, that won't work on me!" she said, flushing. "You'll do your share of the cooking, *friend*, or you won't eat at all."

"Fine!" Kerk threw out his arms and bowed. "Forgive me for having my own opinions, my great and mighty, my 'I'll be just as common as you are' Ruler." He scowled and began kicking around in the bush for kindling.

"I'm not ordering you, Kerk," said Paragrin. "It's just fair practice." She sat down on the grass and began attacking the stick with her knife to sharpen it, wishing it were his too-handsome face she was carving instead of the wood. "Going on this trip together was a bad idea," she muttered.

"You don't have to tell me!" he called back, and Paragrin narrowed her eyes.

4

So. This was perfection. Magramid, standing at the entrance to the Melde Colony, was uninspired. The little stone-and-clay dwellings of the riverside and court were no more than ordinary, and the mortals themselves were just as petty as those of the Vasser Colony—rushing about as they always did, on their own insignificant errands. Magramid was almost disappointed; this would be no sport to destroy. The only real satisfaction she would get would be from knowing that her sister's pride was unfounded.

Especially for Paragrin, thought the Half-Divine contentedly. "Even my city's rulers don't abandon their people."

"You don't know what you're talking about," declared a young man, brushing past her with a round of goat cheese under his arm. "And I don't want to listen anymore."

Magramid's eyes widened as she caught the glint of an Amulet against his chest.

"You have to listen," said his companion, a large woman with a single fat braid down her back. "I mean, you *should* listen, my Ruler. Can't you see the desecration of that old tyrant's being in the House?"

"I said enough, Atanelle. You've made your opinion clear."

Cam hurried ahead of her through the market-day

crowd, but Atanelle pursued him, pushing past an aggressive nut vendor to continue her harangue.

"And you know why Ram's shown up now, don't you?" she said. "Because our Ruler Paragrin is gone! How he even found out she was gone before you and Notts made the official announcement, I find highly suspicious. If she knew he was making himself known again, she'd have me wrap him in chains. And if she knew that he was staying in her home . . ."

"It's my home, too!" said Cam, and stopped abruptly to look at her. "I am well aware, Atanelle, that Paragrin would be handling her grandfather differently, but I have to follow my own instincts now. He's not trying to reclaim his rule or anything; he just wants to stay in the Great House again for a few weeks. It used to be his home, too. Why shouldn't he be allowed in? Anyway, as far as I'm concerned, any wrong that Ram did is far in the past."

"But unforgivable!"

"No," said Cam. "Nothing is unforgivable." He turned from her and went on into the entrance hall of the House. "Grandfather will stay," he proclaimed, "until he breaches *my* sense of propriety, not yours." He strode beneath the tapestries into the dining room—and stopped short. Atanelle came up behind him, wondering.

There was a hearty blaze dancing in the hearth there— unusual for an afternoon—but it showed off the room to a fine advantage. The flickering light sparkled on the glaze of every dish set upon the table, and there were a good many dishes: one with a bread-and-berry pudding, one with a sweet pastry mold, one with a stack of smoked venison and an assortment of seasonal nuts, and another with a bowl of steaming onion soup. Before it all, bathed in the fire's glow, sat Ram, just finishing cleansing his hands in the dish of scented water that Aridda, the Keeper of the House, was made to hold for him. The old man looked up and smiled at Cam.

"Come, boy," he said, wiping his hands on his shirtfront, "there's plenty!"

Cam watched the water stain spread on the embroidered shirt—on *his* embroidered shirt, the best that he owned. He shook his head and retreated back into the hall, taking the goat cheese with him. Atanelle, her eyes as round as the dishes, followed.

"He's even wearing your clothes!" she said, running up the stone steps after Cam. "Aren't your senses breached yet?"

"Atanelle, please . . ."

"All right. All right, I understand. You're just not used to throwing people out. I am. Let me do it for you. Consider it my duty."

"No . . ." Cam leaned against the wall outside his bedroom, hugging the goat cheese in his arms. "It's my duty, not yours. I just—you're right. Paragrin is very good at these sorts of things, so I generally left them to her. Now," he sighed, "I'll have to learn to do them myself."

"Fine," said Atanelle, and went back toward the stairs. "I'm with you if there's any trouble."

"But not today," said Cam. "Don't look at me that way! I will take care of it, just give me time to work it out in my own fashion. Here." He handed her the goat cheese. "Take this to the larder for me, will you?"

24

"Maybe I should leave it on his table," said Atanelle as she took up the load. "It'll end up there anyway."

Cam shot her a withering glance and disappeared into his chamber.

"Why not give him back the Rectangular Amulet while you're at it?" she grumbled, and clambered the rest of the way down the steps.

When she passed again into the dining room on her way to the larder, Ram was just beginning his soup. He was bent forward with intense concentration to sniff the broth, and Atanelle watched him for a moment, exchanging a look with the beleaguered Keeper of the House; then she held the cheese high above her head—and dropped it to the table. Nuts sprang into the air with the impact, and the soup splashed up—very satisfyingly—into the old man's face.

"You imbecile!" he screamed, and started from the table.

"Sorry," said Atanelle, "but you were through eating anyway, weren't you?" She nodded to Aridda, who began stacking dishes.

"I was not," said Ram. "Leave those here." He mopped ineffectively at his chin.

"You were finished," said Atanelle, and stood so close to the spindly man that the blade at her belt touched him.

"You're a freak, you know that, don't you?" Ram hissed, and turned to splatter what was left of the scented water on his face. "No woman should have muscles like yours." He wiped his chin on his sleeve. "You can bully, but you don't have the power to force me out," he said. "I'll be back." He took up his cane and slunk away toward the front entrance to the court.

Aridda folded her arms beneath her bosom, and Atanelle, shaking her head, took up the goat cheese once more and headed for the larder.

Ram got as far as the entryway of the House in his retreat, and then stopped. An old woman stood in front of the entrance, blocking his passage. She was unaware of him, her rumpled neck stretched to examine something above the portal. Ram poked her with his cane, readying a curse, when her eyes suddenly dropped and met his. The curse caught in his throat and he lowered the cane.

"You should be careful where you stand" was all he could manage, and he squeezed past her into the court.

Magramid put a hand on his shoulder. "Pardon me," she said, "but I was admiring this beautiful carving above the door, so lovingly kept from mold."

Ram glanced up at the Oval and Rectangle entwined in stone. "Yes," he said impatiently. "Now let go of me!" He tried to shake off her hand, but her grip tightened.

"You're a clever man," said Magramid.

Caught by the compliment, Ram stopped his struggle. Magramid let her hand fall away from his shoulder, and her eyes, softened now with better manners, looked not as strange to Ram as they had before. Besides, she was a woman of intelligence. Obviously.

"I would love to talk with you," said Magramid, "about what really goes on behind these famous walls. I'm afraid I have a prying curiosity about the great ones; they're so intriguing. You were inside just now. Do you have any special privilege to visit here?"

Ram pulled back, a look of gross indignity on his face.

"Don't you know, woman," he said with a gasp, "whom you're talking to?"

Magramid peered at him, not comprehending, and then all at once remembered the old leader—one of the Melde's most infamous rulers. "Ah, forgive me," she said, and bowed low. "I didn't recognize you. My lights, you see, are not as bright as they used to be."

Ram raised an eyebrow in doubt. "Mine was a glorious rule," he said. "You at least should remember. You're older than I am."

"Yes," said the woman, "much older."

"Well," said Ram, after taking a moment to recover, "as hard as it is to believe, you're not the first to have forgotten me . . . temporarily. It's the way of this idiot world to rush the children into the sun before the parents even get brown. Best plan of all would be never to spawn the ungrateful things. Do you have children?"

Magramid thought for a second. "No," she said.

"You were smart, then. Now, if you still want to have that talk, you could follow me to the tavern. I was about to get something to eat. You could even pay for my meal to make up for the insult."

"If only I could," said Magramid, "but I'm a poor woman and have nothing to trade."

Ram frowned. "What about those necklaces you're wearing?" he persisted, pointing to the delicate chains that curved around her neck and disappeared beneath her clothes. "What's on the ends of them? Something valuable?"

Magramid's eyes hardened. "Nothing!" she said. "Don't touch them."

Ram lowered his finger quickly. "Well, no matter," he said. "But you'll have to stay several steps behind me as we walk along. That at least you could do, to show your humility."

Magramid bowed again. "It would be my honor," she said.

And so in this fashion Ram and Magramid wound their way out from the court and into the narrow dirt streets that surrounded it. They passed through a great many of these paths, each neatly separating comfortable little rows of cottages, but there was evidence hiding in new plaster and recast walkways that the Melde Colony had not always been so comfortable. Not, Magramid was certain, in Ram's time. So. There had been improvement with Cam and Paragrin's rule—but hardly *perfection*, she assured herself.

The tavern, nestled on the outskirts of the colony, was a pleasant place, with large windows and a long, polished bar set up with a gleaming line of mugs. As it was mostly empty now—except for the aleman and a woman in a hooded cloak who sat off by herself—Ram was free to claim his favorite place by the fireside. He settled in and turned to offer Magramid a chair, but she had suddenly deserted him, sitting instead with the stranger. Ram stared at her, incredulous at the rudeness of it all.

"Why are you here, in my colony?" asked Jentessa quietly when her sister had joined her.

"Have you come to give me warning again?" Magramid said. "What astounding persistence you have."

"Why are you here?"

"If it's making you nervous," said Magramid with a smile, "then that is reason enough."

"Have you told anyone, *him*," asked Jentessa, nodding at Ram, "that you are a Half-Divine?"

"No! We've only just met," said Magramid. "Splendid fellow. A fine example of the Melde's taste in leadership. Of course, that was before *you* sailed in and made it perfect."

"You're not going to tell me why you've come, are you?" said Jentessa, leaning back.

"I'm visiting! Simply visiting," returned Magramid. "There's no holy law against that, is there? As long as I keep quiet about all the lovely forbidden knowledge concerning our true natures . . . the existence of other colonies . . . your identity . . ." She reached across the table to draw back her sister's hood, but Jentessa caught her and they each began pressing in upon the other's hand, faintly at first, and then, fingers tightening, forcefully. But there was never any point to these contests, and after a moment they returned their hands to the table.

"It's a pity we're so evenly matched," said Magramid. "Now go away. You can't stop me from visiting. I'm sure you've already tried talking to the Maker, but as usual It was uninterested in my affairs. Am I right?"

"Before I go," said Jentessa, not answering her, "let me just remind you of one little holy law that even the Maker would take interest in if you violated it." Jentessa lowered her voice. "The rulers of my colony—of any colony—are chosen, however 'inappropriately,' with the Maker's knowledge. They wear Its symbols of blessing: the Amulets. And if you *kill* one of them, you will be banished from the Center forever. Without being able to renew your mortal body, your spirit will soon lose its only casing and be left to roam the surface of the earth alone, and suffering, for all eternity—

or you could be exiled to another dimension altogether! Do you understand, Magramid? And this warning doesn't come from me this time, but from the Maker Essai Itself."

Magramid raised an eyebrow. "To be perfectly honest," she said, "your rulers aren't interesting enough to kill." She smiled. "One of them has even wandered away . . . Did you know that?"

Jentessa didn't answer to this, either. She readjusted her hood and rose.

"In short," said Magramid, "I am unimpressed."

"Then leave."

"I would, only I keep thinking there must be something I'm overlooking. I'll stay and explore, for a few days, anyway."

"As you will," said Jentessa. "Just be careful. I would hate to see you raise Essai's wrath."

Magramid laughed. "I'm sure you would," she said, and rose herself as Jentessa disappeared out into the city.

"What," said Ram, who was beginning his new meal of rabbit stew when she joined him at last, "was that all about?"

"That was my sister," Magramid explained. "She wanted to remind me of something."

"Pooh," said Ram. "If you want some of my precious time, you'll have to take it on my terms. I won't have you sitting with other people when I'm here alone, you—you— What is your name?"

"It's Magramid, my leader," she said, "and forgive my impertinence, but families can be so difficult. Surely you understand."

"Well! That I do," said Ram, and dabbed at the stew that was dribbling down his chin. "You can't imagine the horrors

I have to go through, just to get respect from my granddaughter Paragrin. It's shameful."

"I'll want to hear about Paragrin," said Magramid, sitting forward, "but for now tell me about Cam—he's more a mystery to me. What is he *really* like?"

Ram waved his hand in disgust. "He has guts of straw," he declared. "Absolutely no confidence in him. That's Paragrin's side of the business. But that's not too surprising," he said with a sigh, sucking the stew off his thumb. "She's my blood, after all."

5

It *was the morning* of the third day out, and
Paragrin's turn to do the cooking. As Kerk, exhausted from
his labors of spear-fishing, lay threatening to sleep again on
the riverbank, the Ruler of the Melde slid her blade quickly
along the belly of the gasping trout and drew out its entrails,
throwing them into the current.

"My Maker, I hate to do this," Paragrin said with a shudder, and wiped her hands on the grass.

"Just fair practice," Kerk replied.

"I know; but why do the fish you catch always seem to
be slimier? Oh, look." Paragrin raised her lip. "It's still
moving."

"Have you started to notice," said Kerk with a sigh, after
another exclamation had risen from the cook, "that the
scenery never changes? That pine up there, I could swear
we passed it two days ago. And these hills . . . the water
. . . All the same. We could have stayed in one place for
days and never known the difference."

Paragrin dropped the trout on the little wooden grate
she had made high above the fire. "What did you expect?"
she snapped, wiping her hands again. She had no patience
for his boredom. Why couldn't he ever be satisfied?

"I don't know what I expected," he said. "Something. And

this—this is nothing." He rolled over onto his stomach and stared at Paragrin, who glanced back at him, a look of great irritation on her face. "Do you think," he said slowly, "that we should go back?"

"No! Stop it, Kerk," she said. That his thoughts could be so close to her own was infuriating. "There's supposed to be a purpose to this trip, or have you forgotten that? Exploration! Do you think I would have left my duties at the Melde just for a holiday?"

"I don't care why *you* left the Melde," Kerk said. "I left for fun, and I'm not having any fun. I'm frustrated. I miss Ellagette." He flopped onto his back again and glared at the sky. "Same stupid birds," he muttered.

Paragrin pierced the trout with a stick and flipped it. "I thought you were tired of Ellagette," she reminded him. "I thought you said she was demanding and unreasonable—especially about wanting to be Joined."

"So maybe I don't miss Ellagette," said Kerk. "Maybe I just miss women." He sat up on his elbows and eyed Paragrin. "How about it?"

Paragrin's mouth fell. "You are disgusting!" she cried, and started to her feet. "If you think—"

"Oh, relax," said Kerk, and fell back again. "I was only kidding. I wouldn't do that to Cam. Besides," he grunted, "you're not even pretty."

Paragrin stared at him, and then at the muddy curl that dangled in front of her nose. "Rot you," she said through her teeth, and pushed her hair back behind her ear. "You can cook your own fish; I've lost my appetite." She stamped off down to the water and splashed her face and hair.

33

"That's not part of our agreement," Kerk said, sitting up, "whether or not you're hungry. It's still your turn to—"

There was a sudden silence. Paragrin paused in her washing to look back again. "What?" she said.

"I saw something." Kerk jumped to his feet and peered into the forest, his body tense, his hand poised at the knife in his belt.

"Like what? A deer?" Paragrin mopped at her eyes, and came up beside him. "That shouldn't be so—"

"Not a deer. Like a person. A man." Kerk went forward, closer to the woods.

"Don't be ridiculous. The only people on earth are days away at the Melde." Paragrin turned, gathering her hair in her hands to wring it. "I'm surprised you didn't imagine a woman," she said. "A *pretty* one."

"Well, I don't see him anymore." Kerk relaxed the hand on his knife. "Must have been— Aren't you going to finish cooking this?" he said, pointing to the trout.

"Oh, it's done by now, anyway," said Paragrin. "I can't improve on it. I'm not a cook; I told you that."

"I wish Cam were here," said Kerk, poking at the fish with his finger.

"*Me, too,*" said Paragrin.

Kerk shrugged in reply, and began to eat.

Afterward, when the two companions had collected their gear and walked off along the riverbank arguing, the man in the forest dared finally to breathe. He crept out into the sunshine, stole the fish head from the blackened grate, and hurried off in the other direction, toward the Melde.

* * *

Much to Kerk's—and Paragrin's—dismay, the next day proved just as dull to their adventurous spirits. And by the following morning Paragrin was almost ready to give in to their boredom and head for home, when all at once they began to notice that the water, and the land around it, were changing.

"Look how wide the river's getting!" Kerk said. "And shallower, too. See, there's grass growing right in the middle of it there. And there!"

Paragrin frowned as her boots sank into the earth. The ground was getting soft, and not just with mud; there was a nasty, gritty stuff mixed up in it as well. "Everything smells different, too," she said.

Heedless of the muck that was seeping through his trousers, Kerk knelt by the river to drink. A second later, he spat.

"This is awful! There's salt in the water."

"Salt?" Paragrin looked at the river, bewildered, while Kerk wiped the taste from his lips. "How could fish survive in such pollution?"

"Something's surviving." He pointed to a black shape gliding by in the water.

"Let's go farther," said Paragrin, and tugged at his sleeve.

They walked on, veering more and more to one side as the river spread itself flatter; expanding and dividing, it began to isolate large patches of grass and grainy earth in the sun; trees shriveled and fell away on the shore. The companions were so engrossed in the strangeness of it all that it was not until they had walked several minutes that they looked up to see where they were going.

All other strangenesses forgotten, they stopped then, frozen in their tracks; for just a short distance ahead, the land came to an end. *An end!* And nothing lay beyond it but water.

They gaped at the emptiness.

"We've reached it, then?" Kerk said at last in a small voice. "The end of the world?"

"I don't believe it," said Paragrin. "What happened to the land? Oh, my *Maker!*" she cried, then clapped her hand to her mouth. "Kerk," she said, "look!"

His eyes fell to where she was pointing just past them on the shore, and he gasped.

"People . . ." he whispered. "It's impossible! How on earth can they be living *here?*"

6

"*Today,*" *Ram announced,* "I will take you on a tour of the Great House itself, along with the added—and dubious—honor of meeting Cam."

"It's about time," grumbled Magramid. She had spent the last four days in the tavern, a prisoner to the old man's wandering reminiscences. He had gone on and on with a great many "historical" narratives about his own glorious rule—she knew most of them to be fabrications—but he had given her little insight into the present governance. Indeed, Ram seemed the last person who wanted to talk about it. At first Magramid had been amused by his fleeting, biting remarks about the Rulers—certainly he had no more faith in Jentessa's assessment of them than she herself did; but at length she had wearied of his endless tales, and would have dismissed him if he hadn't kept promising her a special introduction to Cam—this alone had kept her. One more day of stalling, she had promised herself that morning, and she would set fire to his wagging tongue.

"Now don't be testy," said Ram. "You should have understood from listening to my own experiences that a ruler's life is never his own. Cam has been very busy, in his ineffective way, and I have not been able to arrange a meeting before. Now, however," he said as he led Magramid into the street, "certain—er—barriers have been lifted and the House is mine to show."

"To be perfectly honest," he continued as they wove their way back through the cottages into the court, "I don't understand your interest in Cam. I've been as frank as possible about his shortcomings. Although, through some accident, he has become Ruler, he is nevertheless as common as—as you are. He was not born to the Royal Family, and he exhibits no special properties that might recommend him. He is a man content to stay under the domination of women: first under Paragrin, and now under that warrior Atanelle. He's apprehensive of real men, hardly the quality one wants from a leader. Now, when *I* was Ruler—"

"There he is," said Magramid, grateful for Cam's appearance near the Great House. "There's no more time for anecdotes. Introduce me. Now."

"I was going to," said Ram, and looked quickly around him for any sign of Atanelle. Satisfied, he strode up to Cam, who was conferring with Notts, and tapped him on the shoulder.

"Son, I have someone who would like to see you," he said.

As Cam turned, the brilliance of the sun stung his eyes. For a second he was blinded; then the face of the old woman materialized before him. He blinked at her, disconcerted, for her eyes seemed to hold the light within them.

"Hello!" she said, and held out her wrinkled hand to him. "I've been so anxious to meet you. My name is Magramid, and—"

The introduction was never finished; a terrified shout rang out then from the riverside, followed by screams. All at once the crowds were in chaos as people tried to spin away from the thrashing fear of an intruder.

There was a wild man loose in the court. A man dirty and unshaven, clad only in a pair of ragged trousers; he was howling with confusion and fright, striking out at anyone who stood in his path.

Magramid's face fell. A heavy anger stole over her and she dropped Cam's hand, wanting to burn the half-man for coming, for ruining everything, for trapping her again. The branches of the forest beyond trembled ominously in a sudden wind.

"What *is* that?" Notts exclaimed, as the swirl of shouting drew closer. Forgetting his duties as guide, Ram gasped and ran to hide in the House.

And then the crowds cleared to the edges of the court, leaving the wild man in the middle, alone—until he turned and saw her.

"*Mother!*" he yelled, and arms outstretched, he ran to her.

Magramid did not move, but Cam did, rushing in front of her to save her. As Magramid drew backward, surprised, the half-man charged into Cam, lifting him up in his arms to throw him aside.

"*Stop,*" said Magramid. "Put him down." And the wild man did, almost gently. The people in the court were silenced.

"My Ruler!" cried Atanelle as she ran, blade drawn, from the crowd.

"No, wait," said Cam, and he looked warily from the man to the mother, uncertain. "Is he your son?" he asked, and Magramid darkened. Her inner voice pressed up at the half-man: *Why?* And he cringed at her anger, falling to his knees to embrace her.

As he fell, the eyes of the crowd rose in front of her, a hundred curiosities challenging the scene; and beside her, Cam was gazing down at the humbled man in pity. Quickly she dropped her hand to her son's shoulder, stroking it.

"Yes," she said, "he is mine." She drew back. "You may punish him if you wish."

Atanelle once more moved forward, but Cam shook his head. "No, he's—he's fine now. He's not—" He leaned down to Magramid's ear and said, "He's not quite normal, is he?"

"No," said Magramid. "An accident."

"Ah," said Cam, and straightened up again. "Well then. Perhaps you—the two of you," he added, as the man embraced his mother more tightly, "would like to come in and rest for a moment in the House, out of these people's sight. This way," he said to the strangers, and motioned them inside.

"You said you didn't have a child!" hissed Ram as they passed him in the hall.

Magramid ignored him.

Outside, Notts stood rooted by the entrance, staring at nothing.

"Are you all right?" asked Atanelle.

"I think so," said Notts. "Just a queer feeling, then . . . a chill."

"Well, it's the season for it," she said, and clapped him on the back. "Come on inside with me. Maybe Ram will have ordered up a fire again for this afternoon!"

* * *

"Now," said Cam, when they were all safe within the dining room, "how can I help you . . . Magramid, you said your name was?"

"Yes." The old woman deposited her son in one of the chairs and sat down herself across the table from Cam to study him. He was not particularly impressive, she decided: his build was fit, but too slight about the shoulders and chest, and his good height only magnified his slenderness. There was a grace about his hands and movements that amused her and struck her as feminine; still, he had risked injury in her "rescue." That had interested her.

"I suppose I should thank you for saving me," she said at last.

"Well," said Cam, "I suppose I should be thanking *you*." He glanced uneasily at the wild man, who was looking unnatural in the polished chair, pulling distractedly at the thick bristle covering his chin. "Had I known he was your son—" said Cam, then laughed. "I'll have to admit I'm a bit confused. Have I seen you before? I've met so many people this last year that I'm afraid faces have jumbled together. Your son, though . . . I'm sure I would have remembered. Where have you kept him so peacefully all this time? Where do you live?"

"I live nowhere," said Magramid quickly, "—and everywhere. I have no real home to speak of."

"You mean that you live on the streets?" asked Cam, dismayed. "How awful! I had hoped that during the renovations we had given everyone shelter who needed it."

"Ordinary shelters wouldn't work for me," continued Ma-

41

gramid, warming to her tale. "My son—he isn't welcome. Although it's only recently he's become so disorderly, still, his appearance frightens people. I didn't want to cause trouble."

"Don't you have any other family?" asked Atanelle, who stood close by the wild man's chair, in case anything should happen. "Someone who would have to take you in?"

"No family," said Magramid, and sighed.

"You do so have family," Ram declared, emerging from where he'd been hiding in the entrance hall. "What about that sister?"

"Sister?" said Cam.

Magramid shot a black look at the old man, then glanced apologetically at Cam. "We aren't on good terms," she explained. "It's as if she were dead to me, and I to her. There's no hope of reconciliation there."

"You two seemed jolly enough in the tavern," said Ram.

Cam rapped on the table. "That's enough," he said.

"Should I remove him?" Atanelle asked cheerfully, and she smiled at Ram, who hissed at her.

"He can stay," said Cam, "if he behaves. I'm sorry, Magramid, but my grandfather—"

"Grandfather-by-a-Joining," put in Ram.

"My grandfather-by-a-Joining," said Cam through his teeth, "has been away from polite people for so long, he's forgotten how to be civil."

"I understand," said Magramid, and Ram, grossly insulted, quit the company to find solace at the tavern.

"My grandfather said that you wanted to see me," said Cam. "What about?"

42

"Nothing specific, my Ruler," said Magramid. "It's just that I've been such an admirer of yours for some time—you and your mate."

"Really?" Cam was pleased. "Well, thank you. I know Paragrin and I haven't been leaders for long, but I had hoped we'd made a good beginning."

"It was my fondest wish," Magramid continued, "that I might touch your hand before I died."

"Oh . . ." said Cam. "I'm sorry. Are you ill?"

"Old, my Ruler. Just very old, and tired." Magramid stooped in her chair, as she had seen other old women do, and Cam gazed across at her, frowning with concern.

"Well," he said after a moment of consideration, "I'm certainly not going to let you sleep outside another night. Notts," he said, beckoning to the man who had been hovering the whole time under the tapestries in the portal, "do you know if that house by yours on the riverbank is still vacant? The tiny one, with the leaky roof? With a few repairs, we could . . . Notts, are you all right?"

The little man hadn't stirred when Cam first addressed him, his eyes fixed all the while on Magramid. Now he broke from his trance, startled, and stared at his Ruler. "What?" he said.

"Notts, come closer," said Cam. "I want you to meet Magramid. Magramid, this, you must know, is our Holy Intermediator."

The old woman turned in her chair and stared at Notts, who had moved forward cautiously. She stretched out a hand to him and he had to take it, his eyes wide at her smile.

"I've heard of you," said Magramid. She said it softly; why did it sound so menacing to him? "You are the human link between the Maker Essai and Its people," she concluded.

"Paragrin and I appointed Notts ourselves," Cam explained, "when Jentessa left."

"Of course! Now tell me," said Magramid, still staring at Notts, "do you have any real enlightenment with the great Maker, my friend, or is it all affected?"

Notts began to speak, but he had to look away from her eyes, stepping back awkwardly from the scene. "I'm sorry, Cam," he said. "I'm afraid I'm not feeling well; the weather, I think. Perhaps I should just lie down for a while . . ."

"Yes! Atanelle," said Cam, "help him upstairs."

The warrior moved forward, but Notts put out his hands. "No. No, thank you, my Ruler; I'll be fine at my own house. Atanelle, don't bother."

"Nonsense," she said. "I'll see you home, at any rate." She took Notts by the arm and led him gently out of the room.

"I'll come by your house later," called Cam, and sank down at the table. "He was acting so strangely . . . Not like himself at all."

"Sensitive, isn't he?" said Magramid, and gazed thoughtfully into the entrance hall.

"Well, I guess we'll have to find another person to help you to a shelter tonight," said Cam.

"Perhaps . . . perhaps I could stay here for now?" she suggested.

"I'd offer, naturally," said Cam, glancing again at the wild man, who was scraping his fingernails along the edge of the table, "but I'm afraid there isn't any room. As soon as Atanelle comes back, she'll have you—"

"No. Don't put yourself out, please," said Magramid. She began to push herself up from the table, laying her wrinkled hands down for support. "I've taken so much of your time as it is that I'm—oh!"

Suddenly her arms buckled beneath her and she swooned forward onto the table. The half-man let out a cry and threw back his chair to embrace her.

"Are you all right?" Cam exclaimed, starting toward her. The wild man warned him off with a snarl, turning again to wail at his mother, when Magramid's eyes focused and she looked about her, terribly embarrassed.

"I'm so sorry!" she said with a gasp. "I don't understand what happened. Please, we'll let you be . . ." She pushed against her son to right herself, stumbling as another fit came over her.

"I can't let you go," said Cam, dancing around the man in an effort to help her. "I'll— Aridda!" he called, and the Keeper arrived from the larder, her hands and face dusted with wheat flour.

"Aridda," he said, "stop whatever you're doing and help me here, could you? This woman has taken ill!"

"Probably all she needs is rest," said Aridda. She folded her arms and looked critically at the strangers. "If this— man—wants to bring her into the back room, I'll see what I can do."

"No—upstairs. Bring your mother upstairs, where it's more comfortable," said Cam, gesturing to the son.

45

"I could help her just as well down here," said Aridda, but Cam paid her no mind. The half-man had swept Magramid into his arms and was following Cam to the stairs, moaning; so Aridda slapped the flour from her hands and trudged up after them.

7

Yes. In the new, strange world of grainy earth and endless water, there were people. *Other* people. Kerk and Paragrin could hardly believe it, could not understand the who or what or why, but there was no denying what they saw. Ahead of them, on platforms that jutted out into the mouth of the river, there were people. They were working, hauling nets of fish from deep wooden rafts to the platforms, where they spilled their catches, still flapping, into baskets. There must have been dozens of rafts tied up there, and more coming in across the water, their broad cloth sails spread like wings to the air.

It was an awesome sight—all of it!—and the travelers from the Melde stared for some time in amazement, until Paragrin's curiosity dared her farther. She pulled on Kerk's sleeve and they moved cautiously forward, leaving the last shelter of shrubbery behind them to stand out near the platforms. They waited there, watching the people ignore them; then they ventured even closer, with eyes round and legs trembling, until Kerk, finding himself near a basket, bent down to inspect it. He pointed at a fish and smiled.

"Look," he said. "Have you ever seen fins like this before?"

Paragrin pulled at him again. "Don't stop now. Let's go

47

farther!" She looked around at the people and the rafts, shaking her head. "This cannot be real," she said.

The two of them walked on, until at length they came to the front of the line of platforms and saw where the people were going with their catches. The land's end met the water on both sides of the river mouth, but it wasn't like a regular meeting: a bank, with clay and rocks and steep grassy mud. It was entirely different. This ground was flat and smooth, angling only slightly when it merged with the water. And stranger still, the ground was all one unnatural color: yellow.

"This is a ground?" said Kerk. "Where's the dirt? What *is* this stuff?"

They stepped uncertainly onto the sand, their feet sinking down among the grains as they moved.

"It's worse to walk on than mud," muttered Kerk, but Paragrin was fascinated and knelt down to collect some in her hand.

"It's cleaner, though," she said, admiring the sparkle on her palm. "And hard. Look, Kerk, it's made up of tiny rocks, so small and pure, as if they had all been washed by the—"

She had stood up to point at the water before them, yet was stopped in her sentence, struck dumb again by that smooth, low horizon. She had never seen anything like this before, had never imagined a different kind of sky that wasn't broken by the sharp tips of pine or the crags of the mountain. At the Melde, everything was vertical; here, it was amazingly flat, endlessly horizontal, and peaceful. The gentle waves offered their foam to the shore and then, with a sigh, fell away again.

"It's as if they were bowing," whispered Paragrin, and Kerk moved up beside her.

"I'm going to touch it," he said, and they went down together.

They stayed by the water for a long time, she kneeling to examine the colorful shards the waves had deposited on the sand, and he discarding his boots to wade into the sea.

"It's cold!" he roared, and she laughed at him; but when another group of people disappeared over a high ridge behind them, the companions decided to follow.

"We'll come back here later," said Kerk. "We have to come back!"

Braving the slippery sand, they stumbled up to the grasses that dotted the side of the ridge. The farther up they went, the harder the ground became, until when the ocean was low at their backs, they stood upon real dirt again at last.

It was then that they saw where the people were going.

Kerk and Paragrin looked at each other, but they could not speak. Below them, spread out in all directions, lay a city.

"Another colony!" said Kerk finally. "Paragrin, can you *believe* it?" He flung his arms around her. "All of this; it's better than anything! Can you imagine their faces when we tell them at home of another colony? Great Maker, I'm glad we didn't turn back!" He gave a whoop and hugged her again.

"Be quiet," said Paragrin, though she was just as excited as he. "We have to be careful. We don't know what it's like here. Don't give yourself away until we—"

"Anything you say," Kerk shouted. "Let's go!"

"Kerk!" she cried as he flew ahead of her down the ridge; but she hadn't the heart to be angry. "Wait for me!" she called, and ran after him into the city.

Crowds! Paragrin never thought she would have missed them. Yet these crowds were different, she told herself; they weren't *her* responsibility. With the Amulet safe beneath her jacket, she ran with Kerk into the streets. That there were houses, amazing! Workshops, astounding! How could the men and women walk so casually through this city?

"It seems as if the Maker took up the Melde and put it down again here," said Kerk, "filling it with strangers."

"It's unnerving, isn't it," said Paragrin, "how similar it is?"

"It has quite a different smell, though," said Kerk, and wrinkled his nose.

There were fish *everywhere*: in people's bags as they walked along; laid out by the dozens in merchants' shops. Through windows came the scent of fish sizzling over fires. Along the streets there were baskets filled with discarded bits of fish—this was the worst—heads and tails that cats crawled over and fought for. There were a lot of cats in the city.

The people themselves, as Paragrin dared to study them, looked different, too. All had a flush about them, a roughness to the skin; even the children had it, and some of the old faces were so coarsened and dark that they seemed like the skin of apples left too long in the sun.

There were a great many people as well, Paragrin saw as she walked through the streets, easily as many as there were in the Melde, and yet there was something very odd about them. What? She looked closer. All of them were busy. She looked for signs of an idler. The Melde certainly had its share: wastrels and rogues who lived more from trickery than honest work; but there was no evidence of such delinquency anywhere here. The only intriguing-looking person she saw was a man who kept close to the edge of the streets, knocking the cats from the baskets with his one good hand.

A horrible thought struck her then: What if this colony were better?

"It *has* got a bad smell to it, hasn't it?" said Paragrin, and frowned.

"Yes," said Kerk, "and it's making me hungry."

Paragrin turned to talk to him, but his attention was caught by a boy with his arm well involved in a woman's fish basket. The woman was arguing with a vendor and was obviously unaware of the child as he eased out a fish from her store. The boy was confident, intent—until he sensed Kerk's gaze upon him and froze, staring back in horror; yet Kerk only smiled.

The boy held his stare, but his expression softened. He finished the catch, slipping the fish underneath his shirt. Kerk laughed and the boy broke into a grin.

"I have an idea," Kerk said to Paragrin. "Come with me."

"Where are we going?"

"To get lunch."

"To get— Kerk, no! What are you doing?"

Kerk had moved in by the woman with the basket on her arm. "Just watch," he said quietly, and winked at the boy standing off now by a shop. Kerk stretched his hand, slowly, toward the fish.

"Oh, my— Kerk . . ." Paragrin saw it all then: the low crime about to be committed. And yet the fish looked so good and she was so hungry. The basket was brimming with food; surely the woman wouldn't mind if—

"Thief!" cried the woman. She had turned suddenly, but Kerk snatched the fish anyway and threw it to Paragrin. The woman struck out at them, shrieking, and Paragrin, deciding to cut their losses, threw the fish back at her and ran. Kerk bounded out beside his accomplice, dodging the people who were all at once everywhere clogging up the streets. The woman screamed above the crowd: "Thieves!"

"My thunder," gasped Paragrin as they ducked, panting, behind a group of men. "She has the fish back. What more does she want?"

Paragrin was just looking out to see if the woman was following, when the small group of men—four, with disturbingly uniform caps—turned and stared at them. She felt her heart sink within her; she backed away, taking Kerk's hand in hers, then made to bolt again into the crowd.

But the men laid hold of them. Kerk struggled with two and Paragrin almost began to fight them as well, using the powerful tricks that Atanelle had taught her. Yet at the last moment she relented; why make more of a spectacle of herself than she had already, over this nonsense? Subdued and deeply embarrassed, she was pulled beside Kerk, with the four officers behind her, as the woman, waving the stolen fish in her hand, pushed through the crowd to indict them.

The next thing they knew, they were locked in a dank little cell somewhere in the city.

"You'll go to judgment tomorrow," said the tallest of the officers. "Count yourself lucky that you have one more night to be whole."

"I wonder what *that's* supposed to mean," muttered Kerk when he had left. "This is so ridiculous! Why didn't you just tell them who you are?"

"Why didn't you just keep your hands out of that fish basket?" Paragrin snapped. "And then—throwing the fish to me, as if it were my idea."

"You would have let them take me alone, wouldn't you?" charged Kerk.

"Well, at least then I might have been able to do something to get you out. As it is, we're both helpless."

"Helpless? All you have to do is show them that Amulet! Why are you being such an idiot? I'll tell them about it myself."

Paragrin seized Kerk by the arm. "You keep still until we learn more what we're up against. For all we know, they'll think we're crazy and do worse to us than we'll get for stealing."

Kerk wrenched his arm free and glared at her. "All right. I won't say anything—for now. But if our judgment tomorrow turns nasty, I'm sure not going to stay quiet for *your* sake."

"Fine! Be stupid," said Paragrin, and she flung herself down in a corner to wait. "Incredible," she said after a moment. "Even their prison smells like fish."

8

"*This* is *amusing*," said Magramid. The morning sun was pouring into the chamber, highlighting the fine tapestry on the far wall and catching in the polish of the bed frame. "To have such a beautiful room," she sighed, drawing up her knees luxuriously beneath the blanket, "for such a simple performance! Look, boy," she said, holding out the embroidered edge of her covers, "have you ever seen such careful work?"

The half-man rose from his own bed—a woven rug by the doorway—and dutifully admired the edge. "The symbol again," he noted, running his finger across the stitching. "Ovals and Rectangles together."

"Yes," said Magramid, her lip rising. "They are pious here, aren't they? That's Jentessa's fault." She pushed aside the covers and rose. "I should have known she'd boast about a man like Cam. He's perfect for her: so gullible and innocent. No natural man, or woman either, should be this untouched by life's deceptions."

Magramid took her two necklaces from beneath the pillow and put them on again, concealing their treasures behind her bodice. She stood before the looking-plate, adjusting the cloth. "I promise you one thing," she said, not so much to her son, who had wandered over to the window, as to her reflection, "this pretty shield from reality that he keeps up around him must be as thin as a petal. One good push . . ." Lost in the possibilities, she took up a comb from the table.

"Put that down!" The curtain into the chamber was thrown aside, and Ram stood in the entryway, a gnarled finger pointed at Magramid. "I have come to collect my belongings, and that is *my* article, specially made. I forbid you to touch it." He marched forward, seizing the comb from her hand. "Bad enough that you steal my room." Suddenly Ram was aware of the wild man by the window, his bulky frame silhouetted, ominously, in the sunlight. "It's just unfair, that's all," he said, "a person of my station sleeping in a smaller . . ." His voice faded as the man started slowly toward him.

"I agree," said Magramid, and pushed her son away. "But what could I do? Our Ruler's kindness was thrust upon me before I could argue."

"So I heard. You seem healthy enough now," Ram observed.

"Better, thank you." Magramid eyed him for a moment, then sat down on the bed, motioning Ram to join her. "Actually, I'm glad you came," she said. "I have a little sport in mind for your grandson, and I think perhaps you can help me."

"A sport?" Enthralled, Ram sat beside her.

"I'll admit," she said, "that I distrust people who claim to be virtuous. It's bad of me, I know, but I find your grandson . . . annoying."

"Grandson-by-a-Joining," Ram reminded her. "And I agree. He hasn't any strength to his character."

"Or perhaps to his convictions," said Magramid. "Is it true

55

what you said before, that he claims he could never kill anyone? That he refuses to engage in fighting, because he thinks it's wrong?"

"Even for self-defense," said Ram. "Can you *believe* it?"

"No," said Magramid, "I can't."

"Really?" Ram sat back, surprised. "I can. He's just that ridiculous."

"Let's put him to a test, then," said Magramid, and her eyes shone. "Let's get somebody to challenge him, someone strong and brainless . . ."

Ram glanced back to the wild man hovering by the window, but Magramid shook her head.

"I don't want our Ruler to think I had anything to do with it. Besides, it's better if the challenger is well known in the city. We should make this as public as possible."

Ram brightened. "I know just the person, and just where to find him!"

"Excellent," said Magramid. "Take me there, and we'll see what we can do."

"But wait," said Ram. "Let's make this even more fun. You and I disagree on the outcome; let's make a wager. If I'm right, if he allows himself to be hit in front of large groups of people, you"—he grinned—"give me back the room!"

"And if his pacifist claims prove hypocritical," said Magramid, "what do I gain?"

"Satisfaction," said Ram, "and full rights, as far as I'm concerned, to stay here as long as you can—until Paragrin comes back, anyway; we're both out then."

"Agreed," said Magramid, and the conspiracy plotted, their old hands wove together in a contract.

* * *

"Wait. I don't understand. He was saying *what?*" Cam was seated later that morning in the dining room, his mouth full of goat cheese.

Atanelle stamped her foot in frustration. "He was insulting you on the open street! What more do you want? I spoke out in your defense, and he started to fight me. All I need is your permission and I'll lock Fratt away forever—after I throttle him."

"What exactly did Fratt call me?"

The warrior studied the floorstones. "He called you—a posy," she said.

Cam stared at her, then broke into laughter. "Sweet Maker, Atanelle, I've been called worse! What's the problem? Why do you care what that idiot says?" He laughed again and took another slice of cheese.

"I wouldn't," she replied, "except he said it loudly, in front of a lot of people. And"—her gaze returned to the floorstones—"and there's been some talk about your inability to rule without Paragrin."

Cam paused in his chewing. "Really? I haven't heard anything."

"You haven't been out among the people much, my Ruler; I have, and it curls my hair to hear your name defiled."

"Well, Atanelle," said Cam quietly, putting aside the plate, "you've got to develop a thicker skin. I can't lock a man up for disliking me."

"At least let me whip him," she pleaded. "I have him right outside. A big crowd has gathered; they want satisfaction, too. I could just give him one pass with my belt. He'll get

57

off smarting but free, you'll have proven your leadership, and everyone—except Fratt—will be happy. And he ought to count himself lucky for your kindness, at that."

Out from the court, the deep voice reannounced its opinion: *"Posy!"* and ripples of laughter floated into the dining room. Cam rolled his eyes and got up from the table.

"This sort of thing disgusts me," he said. "Atanelle, you should never have made this such a spectacle. Now, instead of ignoring him as I should, I have to give in to his challenge. All right. Bring him inside, then. We'll do this as quietly as possible." He ran his fingers through his hair. "I wonder how Paragrin would handle this."

"She wouldn't handle it inside, that's for certain," Atanelle mumbled. "She'd be sure the people *saw* what she was made of."

Cam looked across at the warrior, and his gaze hardened. "I thought you understood my ways, Atanelle. Maybe it's not just Fratt's doubts I need to banish."

Atanelle lowered her eyes. "Just his, my Ruler."

"I shouldn't have to prove myself to anyone," said Cam, and turned away from her toward the door.

When Cam appeared in the court, an eager buzz rose up from the people. He saw then that Atanelle was right: this was no ordinary midmorning crowd. A show had been promised them, obviously, and he was the main attraction—with Fratt.

A blacksmith of impressive brawn and unimpressive brain, Fratt stood between two of Atanelle's soldiers, apart from the crowd. Cam met his eyes. Already the man was wrestling him for control, defying him with the insistent shove of his stare. Cam felt it, and his whole being filled with loathing for this kind of creature. Fratt bared his teeth in a grin, and mouthed the insult again with his lips. Some men around him—his followers—caught the silent irreverence and laughed. Back by the Great House, Magramid and Ram looked on, their faces lit with anticipation.

"He just said 'posy' again," Cam revealed in a loud voice to the people, "just in case you hadn't all heard. Fratt, you might at least have complimented me aloud, then, so that everyone could have enjoyed it; unless, of course, they've grown bored listening to it. I know I have."

"It's the truth!" said Fratt. "You're not a man. Your mate's more man than you are."

Cam felt his cheeks flush, and he cursed himself for letting Fratt get to him. "If that's all you have to say to me," he said, "I've heard it now. Go back to your metal shop and let me get back to my work." He moved to reenter the House when Fratt's voice rang out behind.

"He's a coward!"

Cam closed his eyes. When he reluctantly turned again, he found Fratt playing like a vendor to the people.

"I'd fight him! I'd show him myself who was more fit to be Ruler in Paragrin's absence," said the blacksmith. "But he hides under that Amulet. It gets him protection with the soldiers, so he can do what he wants."

The crowd stirred, weighing the accusation. Ram poked Magramid with his cane. "See? I told you Fratt was perfect for our sport," he said.

"Cam will fight him in a moment," Magramid whispered. "I can see it on his face."

"No, he won't," said Ram. "Watch."

Cam stood exposed before the crowd, agonizing over what to do. He desperately wanted to follow his own intelligence and dismiss the nonsense, but it was becoming suddenly, painfully clear to him that his was a *public* position. The people's faith, however simply they weighed it, was important to keep. Could he trust them to understand his retreat?

It was with a great uneasiness that he realized he could not leave. But there had to be a civilized way to bring Fratt, or more importantly, the people, to his own peaceable way of thinking. A moment more of tense debate, with the expectant stares of the crowd upon him, and Cam knew what he had to do. He took a breath and braced himself, because he understood that once it was begun, he could not back out—not for anything. Cam lifted his eyes and met the blacksmith's glare.

"I have no reason to 'hide,'" Cam said quietly, and without lowering his gaze, he drew the Rectangular Amulet from around his neck. "Atanelle," he said, "hold this and keep your soldiers away. Now, Fratt, I am waiting."

The blacksmith was unnerved by this action and glanced to Atanelle for answers. She had none to give and only looked at Cam, bewildered.

"You're going to fight me?" asked Fratt, amazed.

"There!" said Magramid, and squeezed Ram's arm.

"No. I don't believe in fighting," Cam replied.

"There, yourself," said Ram, and leaving Magramid behind, he pushed forward into the crowd for a better look.

"So what, then?" asked Fratt, confused.

60

Cam spread his arms out from his sides. "I'm waiting. You implied that you'd make a better ruler than I. Show me—show all of us—your great qualifications for leadership."

Fratt was stymied, the people intrigued. Magramid looked about her, uncertain, at their fascination.

"You're wasting my time," said Cam, and he ran his eyes across the crowd, "*and* theirs."

"What do you want me to do?" said Fratt. "I can't hit you if you don't hit back! What kind of fight would that make?"

"Prove what you're able to, or go away," said Cam. Fratt stared at him, then he waved his hand in disgust and turned. Cam's heart lifted; would this be all it needed? He had won, then—without the sacrifice.

Magramid sucked in her breath, cursing. Fratt was a fool! His own followers began to taunt him, muttering among themselves, throwing hisses at their thwarted hero.

Their rebellion was too much for the blacksmith. They'd misunderstood his retreat, so he had to turn back. Before Cam could reach again for his Amulet, Fratt seized him by the arm and spun him around, punching him hard in the stomach.

Cam doubled over onto the ground, the crowd gasped, and Atanelle began to fly at Fratt, but Cam called out her name, stopping her. He pushed himself to his feet, trying not to show how he fought for his breath, and held his arms out at his sides again, ready.

"Now what?" said Fratt, a little shaken by his own defiance.

"You haven't proven yet who was the more fitting leader," said Cam.

"My Ruler, don't do this," urged Atanelle. "Don't be stupid."

"Quiet!" he snapped. "This is between the blacksmith and me. Well, Fratt? Have you had enough?"

Fratt turned again to his followers, but they were no more relenting. "Prove it to him, Fratt!" one shouted. "You said you could show him."

"I *can* show him. I *did* show him," Fratt shouted back, but he made his point once more to them—there the fool was, waiting for it—and Cam fell to the ground for a second time.

Yet he was up again in a moment, less steady than before but just as determined.

"Again?" cried Fratt.

"Unless you're finished," Cam panted. "You haven't beaten me yet."

"Damn you!" Fratt yelled, and felled him for a third time—and a fourth—and still Cam staggered up to confront him.

"Sweet Maker," said Atanelle, as her Ruler swayed on his feet. "At least use those tricks I taught at the Battle! You don't have to hit him, just *defend* yourself."

"Nothing. I'll do nothing to appease this idiot!" said Cam. "Fratt! Are you finished?"

"What do you want me to do?" yelled Fratt, backing away. Cam's eyes were beginning to frighten him. He couldn't stop them from goading him, hating him. *Still* they were demanding satisfaction. One last time, Fratt tried to defeat him, tackling Cam to the ground. "What else do you want me to do?" Fratt cried, beating at him with his fists.

When his passion was spent, Fratt rolled to his feet,

gasping for air. His victim lay below him, face to the ground and silent. Everyone in the court was as quiet, straining their necks to see, horrified by the sudden stillness. Fratt stared down at Cam, his stomach filling with dread.

Magramid pushed to the front of the crowd to see what she could not believe.

Atanelle looked, eyes bulging, from Cam to Fratt and back again. She knelt down by Cam's side, afraid to touch him. The crowd held their breath—and then Cam stirred. His fingers splayed, trembling, against the dirt and he began to push himself up.

"Thank the Maker," said Fratt, and Atanelle put an arm around Cam to help him, but Cam warned her back. She stood apart, and slowly, painfully, determinedly, he got to his feet and turned once again to Fratt.

"No!" said Fratt. "No more. You win!"

"Then go," said Cam, almost in a whisper. "Go home."

Fratt began to back up, but suddenly the crowd broke from its silence, crying out in anger and indignation. It pressed in on the blacksmith, wanting blood for blood.

"Let him go!" Cam shouted, and he held up the Amulet that Atanelle had returned to him. "Because I am Ruler, and it is my more peaceful will that prevails, not his."

The crowd held its stance, then slowly backed away from Fratt, leaving a path for the blacksmith to escape. Fratt stared at the people, stunned, and before he left, he turned to Cam and, with a new respect, bowed his head.

There was silence again in the court as Cam replaced the Amulet against his chest. Then, all at once, the crowd exploded with applause. Cam looked out at the people, surprised. A faint smile broke across his face as he listened to the cheers and the clapping.

"My Ruler," said Atanelle, dropping to one knee, "I will never challenge you again."

"Yes, you will," said Cam and, laying a hand on her shoulder, added to her ear, "but nothing is unforgivable . . ." He turned to receive the cheers one last time; then, finding them too deliciously embarrassing and his body too distressingly painful, he went back into the House to find Aridda and a tub of salve.

Magramid clenched her fists.

"I hope you enjoyed that 'sport' as much as I did," came a voice.

Magramid spun and found Jentessa, wrapped in a cloak, behind her. The woman's fine features were hidden in shadow, but Magramid could tell that she was gloating.

"I'm not convinced yet," Magramid hissed.

"What more will you need?" said Jentessa, and disappeared again into the crowd.

"The room upstairs is mine!" said Ram, skipping back to Magramid's side. "I won the wager."

"You've won nothing," said Magramid, "but my contempt."

She pushed past him to walk off her rage by the river. Ram stared after her, plotting dark, evil revenge with a secret takeover of the chamber—until he remembered the wild man.

"Rot her anyway," Ram snarled. "You can't trust anyone to keep a promise."

9

    At the Vasser, the morning had passed quietly for Kerk and Paragrin in their cell—quietly and hungrily, for no one had brought them food since their imprisonment the day before. By afternoon, Kerk's face was pressed up to the little window, searching for signs of an approaching meal.

"Anything?" asked Paragrin, miserably.

"No," Kerk growled, squinting in the brightness. "All I see is the back of a house and a piece of street corner. There's a man there, selling—guess what—fish."

"Ohh . . ." said Paragrin, and moved away. "I don't want to see another fish as long as I— Kerk!"

Her tone had changed so abruptly that Kerk turned to see what was the matter. The door of their cell had been pushed open, and two of the officers who had arrested them entered.

"Judgment time," said the shorter of the men, and he held out two lengths of rope. While the other stood by holding a knife against their escape, the companions were prepared for their trial, each being made to wear a cord wound around the waist, with only one hand secured behind. At first Paragrin thought the officers had miscalculated the lengths of rope, but as they seemed quite content with letting their prisoners keep one hand loose, she was not going to argue.

Kerk was not as complacent. "This is a stupid way to tie us," he said, "just about what I'd expect from a backward colony."

"Kerk!" said Paragrin.

"And when are we getting something to eat?" he demanded.

"I'm impressed you can think of food at a time like this," said the taller man, who resheathed his blade and gave Kerk a nudge toward the door. "I've seen some screaming by now."

Paragrin looked back at him, wondering, when her own captor pushed her out of the cell.

The business of life burst around them again as the companions were brought into the streets. Paragrin felt practically blinded by the colors, but when she could focus again on the people, she saw their condemning faces too clearly. All her sense of dignity was lost in their eyes. She wanted to tell them: I am a ruler! Yet, even without her caution as an excuse to stay quiet, she hardly felt like a ruler then, and, she had to remind herself, she wasn't Ruler *here*.

"From one end of the scale to the other," she muttered, and was hustled into another street. This one was narrow, with houses leaning in over the alleyway. People moved to stand against the walls as they passed, staring all the while at the prisoners, a few looked on with pity, most with disgust.

When they reached the end of the street, they stopped before a square box of a building. Like the oldest of the

Melde houses, it was made from stone, except for a wooden frame put up around the entrance. There were strange, bony things nailed to the frame and Paragrin, as she was taken past them through the doorway, could only guess at their original nature. Something familiar about their shapes teased her mind, but she dismissed it as she and Kerk were stopped, finally, in a room.

Although there was a raised desk before them, Paragrin couldn't see who was sitting at it. It wasn't so much the height of the desk as the reintroduction to darkness that hindered her vision. The only light spilled in from the entrance, and this was quickly dimmed as the tall man drew a curtain across it.

All at once a lamp was lit at the desk. The sudden flame made Paragrin jump, and as she tried again to see who sat there, she found the brightness more impenetrable than the dark.

"So what have we today?" came a voice from behind the light. It was a woman's voice—almost a friendly one—and Paragrin's heartbeat quickened as she realized who the woman must be.

"You're a ruler, aren't you?" she exclaimed, shielding her eyes with her hand.

The woman laughed so abruptly that Paragrin knew she had been wrong. One of the men made a noise in his throat.

"Now. Enough stalling," said the voice. "What's the offense?"

"Theft," came the answer.

"Child? Boat?"

"Fish."

"Maximum penalty," said the woman. She laid a thick reddish towel across the desk.

Kerk and Paragrin's free hands were placed on top of the towel. The companions looked at each other, not understanding, as the officers positioned an arm around their shoulders, bracing them.

"Oh, my Maker!" gasped Paragrin, for it was then that she knew what was nailed to the frame of the door. The edge of an ax blade glinted as it rose above her hand on the desk.

"*No!*" She tried to yank her hand away but, failing that, kicked her leg out behind. The officer wailed and released her, and she snatched her hand back again just as the blade swung down to imbed itself in the towel. Paragrin propelled herself at Kerk's captor, distracting him long enough so that Kerk could join her in the fight, swinging out a punch with his free right hand.

"Enough!" barked the voice. "Stop them."

Paragrin kicked again, striking one of the men on his jaw. If only her second hand wasn't bound she could really use her skill, she thought miserably; flip him over her shoulder as Atanelle had once taught her—defeat him easily. As it was, she was too off-balance, too handicapped, and poor Kerk with nothing but regular fighting at his disposal was subdued even more quickly than she.

As his hand was forced again to the towel, Kerk began to confess everything at last: "But we're not even from this awful colony! We didn't know about the punishment!" he yelled.

The woman, easing her ax from the cloth, seemed bemused. "Really?" she said. "And which other colony are we from this time? The Melde?"

Paragrin was so surprised by the mention of her city that she stopped resisting completely, and the shorter man dragged her back into place.

"Yes!" said Kerk, without wondering how the woman knew. "And we don't punish thieves this way. Never."

"I understand," said the woman, "and I congratulate you on your woodsy costumes; it's almost believable." The edge of the blade glinted again, this time poised for Kerk's hand.

"Stop!" he shouted. "Ask *her*! She's the Ruler. Show them the Amulet, Paragrin. Show them!"

The blade paused. "Amulet?" said the voice.

Paragrin looked from the blade to her companion, uncertain. "Yes, I have an Amulet," she said after a moment. "It's the Oval, the symbol of—"

"Where?" And suddenly the blade was withdrawn. Kerk let out his breath, and the woman leaned forward from behind the light to reveal herself for the first time. She was a wiry woman with little eyes, and Paragrin did not like the intensity in her voice. "Where? Show it to me."

When Paragrin didn't answer, Kerk stamped his foot. "My Maker, this is no time to be modest!"

"It's under my jacket," she said. "If you release us both, I'll show it to you."

The woman made a face and reached down. Forewarned, the officer had a firm grasp of Paragrin now and the woman drew the Amulet out from her jacket. With the chain stretched up to the desk, the woman turned the Oval over in her hand. When she looked out again, her expression had changed.

"Open the windows," she commanded. "I want more light."

Kerk's officer moved about the room, unfastening shutters. As the sun streamed in at last, the wiry woman blew out the lamp on her desk and frowned. Paragrin did not like her any better in the daylight.

When the tall man returned, the woman pointed to Kerk. "Search him," she said.

The officer ran his fingers along Kerk's neck, but Kerk pulled away. "I don't have an Amulet!" he said. "I'm not a ruler; my brother is."

"And where is this brother?"

"Where else? In the Melde."

"All right," said the woman, screwing her eyes so much they seemed to disappear altogether, "how long have you been consorting with Magramid? What damning contract did you strike with her so that she would give that Amulet to you? Or have you been working with her all along to undermine our leaders? Tell me!"

When the companions looked back at her blankly, the woman slapped her palms upon the desk. "Enough," she said. "This is out of my duty." She glared at the officers. "Take them to Hanna and Giles!"

"Now where?" groaned Kerk as he and Paragrin were pushed back into the street. A crowd had gathered and stared at the prisoners' untouched hands before hurrying back to work.

A small boy lingered by the entrance, and both amazed

and relieved by this miraculous saving, he set out to follow the prisoners to their next destination.

The two companions were pushed back through the streets toward the city center. With both her hands now tied, Paragrin stopped paying attention to the stares she and Kerk were receiving; she was too busy brooding over the twist their fates had taken.

Why had the Amulet caused such alarm? Who was this Magramid with whom they had been accused of plotting? And where were they going now? "Hanna and Giles" . . . Rulers perhaps, this time, but she was determined not to ask; she would wait to see some visible sign of power similar to her own. Of one thing she was very certain: what had started as a rightful arrest had turned quite another color. Now the trial was over, her identity known, and *still!* Angrily, she pulled against the ropes that bound her, and when the officer urged her on with a particularly unfriendly push, she stopped dead in her tracks and knocked him in the chest with her head.

She was neither surprised nor cowed when he seized her by the collar; she met his scowl and returned it, ready for anything but submission.

"Traitor," said the man. "I'd take care of you myself if we hadn't the Two. They'll do what's right, and better."

Behind her Paragrin heard a door being opened from the street. She tried to twist in his hold to see where they were going, but the officer half lifted, half dragged her through the doorway, finally casting her to the floor when they were inside.

She broke the fall with her knee. With a groan, she turned over onto her stomach and lay still.

A man's voice then: "What *is* this?" An older man.

When Paragrin raised her head, she saw a set of crooked toes confronting her. The man was standing so close she thought he was about to help her up. He was not.

The sound then of a wooden spoon being dropped against a kettle rim. This time a woman's voice, and a cross one. It said, "You had better have good reason to disturb us here." A pause. "Is it murder?"

"Worse," said an officer, "betrayal," and at last Paragrin was hauled up beside Kerk, where she swayed, glaring at the two new people before her.

New, but not new. The people holding court in the little kitchen room were in their middle years. Although they were both of an age, only the man was well preserved: the hands that grew as gnarly as the toes were strong and capable, and his body—though small for a man's—was fit. His face, crowned as it was by a frizz of receding red hair and anchored by a strip of beard along the jaw, might have seemed comical, if his eyes had not been so sadly knowing, his skin so lined and weathered.

The woman could not be so intelligent, for after noticing the roundness of her chin, Paragrin dismissed her as being soft and self-indulgent. Yet it was she who wore, suddenly, the more dangerous face; for the man's gaze was only angry, hers was mocking.

"Traitors?" she said. Her eyes summed up the prisoners and condemned them, cruelly quick.

Paragrin scowled.

"We're not traitors," said Kerk. "We're not even from here. We're from the Melde!"

"The Melde, is it?" A thin smile crept over her face. "Well, we haven't heard that one in a while, have we, brother Giles?"

"We caught them stealing fish," said the tall officer; "yet it was at the Lower House that we discovered the plot. They're admitting nothing, but the girl has the proof."

Hanna's gaze settled on Paragrin. "This child has something to show us besides her frown?"

"Plenty," said the officer, and reached for the Oval, which had slipped back beneath her jacket. Paragrin butted him away, but when he had regained control of her, Hanna came closer, her eyes wide and wary, and drew the chain and its charm into the light.

A look of intense confusion leapt to Hanna's face when she saw the Oval Amulet: passionate confusion, full of horror and joy and pain. She clutched the Amulet and raised her eyes to Paragrin, where they turned suddenly bright and vengeful.

"You villain!" she cried, and brought the flat of her hand up to Paragrin's cheek.

Kerk pushed forward, but an officer was on him instantly, dragging him away and forcing him to his knees. The other was busy with Paragrin as the woman, determined, wrenched the chain from around her neck and took it for her own.

"I don't understand any of this!" exclaimed Paragrin, landing hard on the floor next to Kerk. "I don't know why my Amulet is so hateful to you. I don't know why you're treating us like criminals, but know this! The Maker Essai is in that Amulet; I have Its blessing as Ruler of the Melde, and every second that you keep it from me, you are committing blasphemy!"

"Blasphemy? *Frut!*" Hanna swore. "Take them away before I slap her again."

As the two were snatched up, Giles folded his arms across his chest. "Chain them to the Wall," he rumbled. "We'll keep them there until they confess the plot." He glanced at the tall officer. "Only the one Amulet?" he asked softly, and the man nodded.

When Giles turned back to his sister, she had tears in her eyes. That was the last thing Paragrin saw before being pulled from the room.

By the time the sun began to set, Paragrin and Kerk were secured and abandoned at the Wall, an outdoor prison made from a thick plank of wood nailed across two tree trunks. It stood high on the ridge that overlooked the sea, but not even that pretty view was allotted them for comfort; they were chained facing the other way, with nothing but the colony below to contemplate.

They were quiet now; there was nothing else they could fight against. Kerk crossed his arms on top of the board, his wrist chains jangling as he moved. He rubbed his face with his hand and glanced over at Paragrin. She had said nothing since their confinement. She had hardly even stirred.

"Are you all right?" he asked.

She turned slowly and stared at him. "If being stripped of my Amulet and then chained to a board is all right, I'm all right," she said. "How are you?"

74

"Try not to think of your Amulet," suggested Kerk. "Be grateful you still have two hands."

When she didn't reply, Kerk heaved a sigh. "Well, anyway," he said, "what's a second night spent as a starving prisoner? All the more color when we tell everyone our adventure back home. This has to be the worst of it."

Just then a thin drizzle of rain began to fall.

"Wonderful," said Paragrin.

10

After his difficult morning with the blacksmith, Cam had looked forward to a restful day, basking in his newfound sense of public regard. He had about five hours of it before life in the Melde was turned upside down.

Just when all the colonists were settling down to their suppers, the earth beneath their feet began to tremble. It wasn't much at first, enough to make the soup in their dishes ripple and sleepy dogs open their eyes; but then the shaking grew stronger. Plates that were hung upon walls broke free from their bondage, shattering. People lost their balance and fell to the ground. Trees shook, and the frailer foundations of the wooden homes threatened to break apart and collapse. Within minutes, the Melde was in chaos.

Cam started up from his own table, eyes wide, grasping the chair for support. Magramid sat across from him, the sullen expression she had worn all afternoon broken by a watchful smile, as Cam's own face went from contentment to horror.

"What's happening?" he cried, as Ram—gone even paler than usual—laid hold of the ale jug to keep it from falling. The wild man hunched suddenly in his chair, his mouth fallen open.

"Mercy!" Ram squeaked, pressing the jug to his body.

The tapestries danced on the walls. Sounds of pottery crashing erupted from the larder as Cam pushed himself into the entrance hall, peering out into the court.

"Oh, my Maker," he said.

Magramid smoothed the linen napkin in her lap, admiring the embroidered edge.

Cam stood for a moment, paralyzed, at the entrance, and Magramid felt his fear invigorate her soul. He would prove a coward yet! When he staggered back into the dining room, she dropped her napkin and fell upon him, clutching his shoulders. "Good—stay!" she told him. "You must protect yourself here. Let the others fend for themselves. For the sake of the Melde, the Ruler must stay safe!"

"Rulers first!" Ram agreed, and threw himself flat on the floorstones, ale jug in hand.

Cam pried Magramid off from him, replacing her in the chair. "You're right," he said. "This is the safest place. Aridda!" he shouted, and the Keeper stumbled out from the larder. "Change this room into an infirmary. There're going to be people who need your help."

He turned and made his way into the entrance hall.

"Great Ruler!" called Magramid, but Cam didn't hear her. Atanelle, coming in from the court, had claimed his attention.

"This is crazy," she said, falling back against the wall with a knocking of limbs. "I never thought we'd feel the likes of this again."

"Atanelle, we haven't another moment to lose," said Cam. "Have your soldiers report—"

"Already reported, my Ruler. They're waiting outside."

"Good," said Cam. "Disperse them throughout the city—especially on the outskirts, where the weaker houses are. We have to rescue people if they're trapped, and bring them here if they're injured. All healthy people we'll enlist with us, or send them back here to help. And we'll have to look to the animals in the barns!"

"My Ruler!" Notts suddenly burst into the entryway, stumbling headfirst to sprawl at Cam's feet. "The omen!" he gasped, as Atanelle helped him up. "The judgment of the Maker Essai is come upon us at last."

"What are you talking about?" asked Cam. "That's nonsense."

Behind him the Half-Divine had come to watch the scene, standing—strangely unaffected by the shaking—in the dining-room portal. Notts cried out when he saw her, his feeling of terror rising.

"Paragrin left and the Maker's condemned us!" he said, grasping at Cam. "I knew it was wrong. You should never have let her betray her duty. I should never have let her, for now It will punish us all."

"Nonsense," said Cam again, but the idea had struck him. A year ago at the Battle, the ground had shaken like this. "The earth is an extension of the Center," Jentessa had said; but the Maker's judgment had helped them then. *Was* this another message? Had the Maker Essai, angry with Its leaders above, sent forth a trembling from the Center to tumble down the city?

Another quake, stronger than the rest, sent Notts sprawling again and Cam and Atanelle dancing to find their balance.

"I can't believe this is a punishment," said Cam. "I won't believe it. You don't believe it either, Notts. We need your prayers, not your panic. If the Maker has anything to do with this, it will be with our salvation. Atanelle, let's go!"

The two were off, running as best they could to meet the soldiers in the court. Notts pulled himself to his knees, trying valiantly to squelch the foreboding in his mind, when he looked up to find Magramid watching him. His hands poised for prayer, he froze, and she scowled down on him darkly, before hurrying out in the night after Cam, the wild man at her heels.

All night long, Magramid followed Cam and his staggering teams of rescuers along the streets. All night long, she watched how he directed the salvation, how he propped old buildings threatening to tremble apart from the earthquakes, how he spread his damnable faith in the inevitable good from doorway to roadway, until he had all but stripped the terror from her magic.

Oh, how she hated him.

Magramid cursed his name as she moved back through the shuddering city, through the patches of torch fire and darkness to the Great House. Cam was so remarkably, so confusingly incorruptible! She could not understand it. But one thing she did know: Jentessa was right about him. Jentessa had won! And this knowledge galled her more than she could bear.

The earth shook again at the mere thought of Jentessa,

and the wild man whimpered in despair. He had followed the follower all night, his legs turning to water with the shakes, and now he reached out, sobbing, to grab her skirts as she entered the House.

"Let me go!" she hissed.

Inside, bathed in the glow of fatlamps braced upon the mantel, Notts was leading prayer in the dining-room infirmary. Magramid paused in the entrance hall to watch him, her lip curling with disgust.

"Fool . . ." she breathed. "Pray to me, if to anyone. The mighty Maker is not responsible this time."

Notts looked up, and even through the dimness of the hallway, he knew it was Magramid standing there. He faltered in his words, seeing her knock her son away with her hand. Clenching his fists, Notts looked down again, continuing his appeal with more fervor, trying not to let his fear and loathing of her vulgarize his prayer.

The tapestries, their bright colors faded to grays in the night, rippled against the walls with every shudder. Magramid moved slowly toward the stairs, feeling the exhaustion of defeat, when all at once she sensed someone hovering in the shadows. Her heart caught in her throat; she sprang for the bottom step, but Jentessa shot out her arm and seized her.

"Has he convinced you yet?" she demanded.

Magramid pulled away from her grasp.

"He's everything I said he was!" Jentessa said. "Admit that you were wrong: hypocrisy does not infect all things. There *is* true nobility . . ."

"In him, perhaps!" said Magramid, "but not in *you*. Let—

me—go!" The half-man had hold of her skirts again and Magramid threw him down. "Damn you all!" she said, and flew up the stairs.

The wild man pinned himself to the wall, his eyes wide upon the fearsome other she had left him with. But Jentessa wasn't thinking about him; her triumphant smile diminished, she stared into the black hall above. The wild man bolted past her, escaping up the stone steps to find his mother.

The rest of the colony held its breath, every living body poised for another quake. Moments passed; curtains that hadn't known rest for hours drifted slowly back into place. The ale inside the tavern barrels stopped gurgling. Dogs looked up from their drool, and there was a silence then in the Melde so profound that only the memories of motion rang in the ears.

The earthquakes had stopped.

As every new minute continued in peace, great shouts of joy and thanks rose up from the city, only to grow more noisy and more exuberant as more disbelievers joined the ranks of the celebrants. It was a glorious hour, and people, giddy with relief, laughing at how their legs still shook, sank down to the gentle ground and embraced their families.

"Notts!" Cam exclaimed, bounding back to the Great House at last. "We've done it. It's over!"

"Bless you," said Notts, hurrying out into the entrance hall with a fatlamp to greet him. "You've done a remarkable job, Cam. Not one death in all this misery."

"Don't thank me," returned Cam, his face shining in the light. "Thank the Maker. I told you It wasn't angry with us. The quakes have come and gone—they weren't a punish-

81

ment, after all. Some scary phenomenon of nature that the Maker put an end to, thanks to your prayers. All's well!"

Suddenly a scream exploded from above. The men looked at each other, then scrambled for the stairs. "It's Magramid," said Cam.

But it was not. Crumpled on the rug in the second chamber, the wooden table broken around his head, lay the wild man. The fatlamp shone upon the blood that trickled down his brow to collect in his lips before dripping off.

"Oh, Sweet Maker," said Notts, raising the lamp tremulously to the attacker. "What have you done?"

Magramid, her wrinkled hands still clenched at her sides, stared blankly at her silent son, as if surprised to find him lying there.

"You've killed him," Notts whispered. "I saw you strike him before, and now you've killed him. You're a perversion of motherhood, a monster!" he cried, and shook the fatlamp at her face.

"Now, Notts, be careful," said Cam.

Roused from her stupor, Magramid lashed back. "Of course you condemn me," she growled at Notts. "You *deserve* to be a holy man. You're as hypocritical as the rest of them."

"Both of you, enough!" said Cam, and wrested the fatlamp from between them. "Aridda, thank goodness," he said as the Keeper appeared with another light at the doorway. "There's been an accident."

"Accident!" said Notts, as Aridda bent toward the victim. "He's been murdered."

"He's alive," said Aridda; "just out from the blow."

"But still, she tried to kill him," said Notts. "She has to be stopped. She has to be arrested!"

"I said *enough*," said Cam. "Aridda, tell Notts what you need from below. You can care for the man here. I'm taking Magramid into my room for a talk."

"A talk?" cried Notts. "She has to be arrested, taken from this House. She's cursing it!"

Cam set his jaw and pulled him aside. "Where is your mercy?" he said. "This sick woman needs our help, not our judgment. Remember, nothing is unforgivable."

"Oh, Cam, be careful," said Notts, shaking his head. "All the world is not as innocent as you."

Cam frowned at him, then held out his hand defiantly to Magramid. She took it, and followed Cam into his room, leaving Notts behind, flushed with his own helplessness.

"You're not going to punish me, are you?" she said to Cam when they were alone.

Cam set the fatlamp on the table and pulled down the blanket of his bed. Behind him the paling moonlight spilled onto the floorstones. "We won't talk about it now," he said quietly. "It's been a terrible night. You must be exhausted."

"I am worn," admitted Magramid.

"Then come," Cam insisted, "and sleep."

Magramid let him help her into bed, all the while staring at him, amazed, her natural suspicion of his kindness doing battle with a new sense of wonder.

"I do not understand you," she said at last, as he sat down beside her. "Isn't it normal to condemn such violence? *I tried to kill my son*," she said, uncertain he had fully realized her sin.

"I know," said Cam. "I know what you tried to do in that moment. You regret it already, don't you?"

Magramid said nothing, still caught in the spell of his gentle voice, that face that looked down filled with— what?—compassion? For *her*?

"Sometimes," said Cam, struggling not to offend, "there are . . . special considerations one has to weigh before giving punishment. Sometimes people do things that they themselves don't really comprehend."

"Am I that special?" asked Magramid.

"Yes," said Cam. "I think so . . . and it won't help to discipline you."

Magramid's expression tightened, and she reached up slowly to touch his face. "All I've ever wanted," she said, "is to be accepted. I've never been accepted by anyone, but especially not by the Maker."

Cam's eyebrow rose. "Not accepted by the Maker? Don't be ridiculous. The Maker Essai loves everyone," he said. "Where did you get such a notion?"

Magramid's hand sank again to her side. "You don't understand," she said.

"Maybe you should talk to Notts," said Cam, brightening. "He could set you straight on this. Surely you would see—"

"No! Not him . . . He knows nothing." Magramid gazed back at Cam, his confusion making her smile. "You are better than he is, don't you know that?" she said softly. "Because you *have* accepted me, haven't you?"

"Of course I have," said Cam. "And I want to help you."

Magramid reached for his hand and, pressing it to her old lips, kissed it. "You've already helped me."

Behind them, a cloaked figure drew back the deer-pelt curtain, her eyes widening as she took in the scene.

"I am sorry for what I did," said Magramid.

"I know you are."

"You are special, too," said Magramid.

Cam laughed. "Thank you," he said. "Now it's time to rest. It's going to be dawn soon!"

"What about you? Won't you rest?"

"I'm afraid I won't get to sleep for hours yet," said Cam with a sigh. "One of those unfortunate quirks of leadership—there's always something to be taken care of."

"Well, things will get better very soon," said Magramid. "Trust me." Her eyes shone then in that strange way they had when Cam had first met her in the court. He felt discomfited again, and got to his feet, glancing away from the eyes.

"Good night," he said. "We'll talk more tomorrow."

"Of course we will," said Magramid. "And relax! Everything's going to be fine now. I promise you."

She turned over and closed her eyes, shutting off their light. Cam looked back at her then, trying to unpuzzle that "specialness," while outside, the cheerful cries of the colony rang through the air.

But Jentessa, who had slipped back into the hallway, was deaf to the celebration. Magramid's behavior confounded her, and she did not like confusion. Especially when it involved her sister—and her gentle Cam.

11

At *the Vasser Colony,* the night deepened; the rain fell hard against the waves and the sand and the two prisoners chained at the top of the ridge. At first they tried to shield their faces, but this was only partly successful; their hair collected so much water that it poured down their noses regardless, and after a time they were so soaked it didn't matter anymore. In fact, when Paragrin spotted the fatlamp coming up from the city, Kerk had thrown back his head and was letting the rain dance onto his face.

"There's someone coming."

He looked down, wiping his eyes on his sodden sleeve. "Why do you think they want us?" he said.

Paragrin shrugged, and her body convulsed with shivers. "Not to give us food or blankets, I'll wager."

"One of them's a girl," said Kerk.

He was right. As the two came to the top of the ridge, the one with the fatlamp held it aloft, illuminating her face as well as the prisoners'. Paragrin made no other observation of her apart from her gender and the fact that she was dry. She had the most wonderful hood attached to her cloak.

The girl peered at Paragrin suspiciously, while the officer stood behind her.

"This is the one," she said. "Unlock her hands from the Wall, but tie them with rope when you've finished. I don't want any trouble. And keep her ankles chained!"

Paragrin let the man prepare her, savoring the warmth when his hands brushed against her skin.

"Where now?" she asked the girl.

"You'll see soon enough," came the reply. She frowned when Paragrin shivered again. "It's drier than this, though, I can tell you that much."

"What about me?" Kerk demanded. "Am I just supposed to wait here until you call again?"

"That's exactly what you're supposed to do," snapped the girl. She turned to peer at him, holding the lamp to his face.

Kerk flinched in the light and screwed his eyes shut, but the girl was struck by his beauty in spite of his contorted state. She stood that way for several moments before Kerk pulled back on his chains.

"Move the lamp, will you? You're blinding me!"

"Oh, sorry!" The girl held the lamp to one side, and Kerk opened his eyes. They were handsome eyes, the darkest and deepest of any she had ever seen. Kerk stared back at her, perplexed, but then he understood: he had seen that look before. He leaned as far as he could across the wooden board and smiled, his wet face shining in the light.

"I'd like to get dry, too," he said softly. "And I'm awfully hungry."

"Meridor, your mother and uncle are waiting," said the officer.

The girl nodded. "I'll come back soon, I promise," she said to Kerk.

"Come back with *food*," he said as the three of them started toward the city.

As the light of the fatlamp traveled away down the ridge, Kerk saw the girl turn and look back at him twice. He waved as well as he could, and when they had all disappeared among the buildings, he blew the air from his cheeks in a long sigh.

As time passed, Kerk had to accept that neither blankets, food, nor sleep were in his near future. He had resigned himself to all that. The one thing he could *not* accept was the boredom of being alone. He gripped the wooden plank and yelled his frustration. That felt good. He yelled again, listening to the sound of his voice die in the falling rain, and then the need for a song overwhelmed him all at once and he belted out a note—this felt as good as the yelling and was easier on the ears—so he began on the spot to compose a sad melody, full of pity for a poor wretch left in the rain. He was just getting to a particularly mournful part when he felt something touch his leg. He stopped the tune abruptly, pulling back on his chains.

"What is it?" he said, peering down at the blackness. The thought that a wild animal might have come upon him in this helpless state made his heart skip, and he yelled again, kicking at the air.

"Wait! It's me," said a voice.

Kerk stiffened, his ankle chains clinking to a stop. "Who's me?"

Suddenly a face rose up to greet him. It didn't rise far, only just above his belt. He stared down, baffled.

"You saw me take the fish, remember?" said the boy.

Kerk brightened. "Oh, you!" he exclaimed, then colored. "I don't usually get caught like this, you understand."

"I was surprised you tried on someone who'd just been plucked," said the boy. "Anyone knows that's a sucker's risk."

"I know that," said Kerk.

"So how comes it that you weren't chopped?" The boy stretched his fingers to the top of the board, feeling Kerk's hands. "Are you a murderer?"

"No!" But when he sensed the boy's disappointment, he added, "At least not of good people; I've killed my share of bad ones, though."

"Really?"

Kerk nodded. "Someone has to take care of them."

"That's right," said the boy. "So why are you here?"

"Ah, a mistake, that's all. You don't want to hear about it." Kerk looked down at the little face, as slick with water as his own. "What are you doing out in this weather?" he chided. "You'll catch cold. You should go home."

"You're tough enough to take it," said the boy.

"Well, I don't have much choice in the matter, do I?" said Kerk, pulling on his chains.

The boy sneezed.

"There! I told you so. Now go on home."

"Why are you trying to get rid of me?" the boy accused,

backing away. "I don't *have* a home, so there, and can do as I please. I warrant you're a traitor, aren't you? A turnabout! One of old Magramid's thuggies. They don't put people at the Wall for just anything."

"And what are you—a spy?" said Kerk. "Then I'll tell you what I told the others: How can I be a traitor, I'm not even from this rotten city!"

"Ho, you're not!"

"I'm not! I'm from the Melde. Oh, why am I arguing with a child?" Kerk leaned against the board, closing his eyes. He was so tired.

The rain fell harder, splashing down his neck and into the boy's face as he frowned up at the prisoner.

"Well, maybe I believe you," said the boy at last. "After all, I've never seen you before, and I know just about everyone in the colony. Besides, your skin looks funny. Is everybody in the Melde so pale?"

"How do you know about the Melde?" asked Kerk. "I'd never even heard there was another colony before."

"Really?" The boy made a face. "Everyone knows about the ten."

"The ten?"

"The ten colonies, you mudhead!"

"*Ten* colonies? Oh, my Maker . . ." Kerk slouched against the wooden plank, his hands pressed to his head. "I don't understand anything anymore. But have you actually seen— Hey!" The little face had disappeared and Kerk looked around, confused. "Don't leave," he called. "I believe you!" Then he felt a tug at his ankle chain and peered down. "What are you doing?"

"Just unlocking these, if you want me to."

Kerk's eyes widened. "You can do that?"

"Sure, it's easy." The boy made a few quick movements and the ankle chain fell heavily to the ground.

"I can't believe you could do that!" said Kerk. "Oh, that feels good . . ." He moved his legs apart, stamping the blood back into his feet. "Now get up here and see what you can do about my wrists."

The boy shook his head. "Those aren't so easy," he said with a sigh. "I tried digging them out from the wood once when I was little and this old man I liked was up here for murder. Is that board in front of you chipped?"

Kerk felt it. "Yes!"

"Well, that's as far as I got, and the old man couldn't pull free. The officers came and he was killed the next day."

Kerk stared at the boy. "Get up here and dig. I can pull better than an old man. Have you got a strong knife? They took mine."

"Sure." The boy scrambled up one of the tree trunks and climbed over to straddle the board in front of Kerk. He took a blade from under his shirt and began chopping at the wood.

"Hey. That's my knife!" said Kerk.

"It is? I took it off one of the officers."

Kerk gazed at the boy in admiration. Not only was he clever but he was good-looking, too, with the same curly dark hair as his own.

"You're all right," he said, and shook the boy's hand. "My name's Kerk. What's yours?"

"Boon," said the boy.

91

"Well, Boon, if you didn't have a home before, you can have one now—right by my side."

The little boy's face lit up with pleasure. "I'll get you free from here, Kerk," he said. "Just you wait and see!"

Down in the city center, where almost every building was dark and only the faithful smell of fish hovered in the corners, Meridor led her prisoner toward the house at the end of the street. Paragrin, stumbling with the chain between her ankles, followed slowly behind with the officer, brooding. Why had she been summoned and not Kerk as well? Perhaps, she thought grimly, they would be questioned about this mysterious "plotting," one at a time, her beaten body brought back to him as an incentive to cooperate.

When they came to the house, Meridor turned and shot a smile at Paragrin. "There's a blanket for you inside," she said, "and one for your friend, too. Is—is he yours?"

"My what?"

"You know," said Meridor, and in the glow of the fatlamp Paragrin could see that she was blushing.

This was so different a train of thought from the one she had been studying that Paragrin could do nothing for a moment but gape at the girl, dumbfounded. "No," she said at last; "he's just a friend."

"Oh!" said Meridor, and turned quickly away, pushing open the door. "Here's the girl you wanted, Mother," she announced. "Did you know there's a boy at the Wall, too?"

Hanna rose from the table, her eyes fixed on Paragrin. "Be silent, Meridor."

"But he's hungry. Can't I just—"

"Sit."

Meridor slammed the fatlamp on the table and sat, while the prisoner stood once more before the Vasser leaders. Paragrin shivered and hoped that the water streaming from her clothes would rot their wooden floor. Looking around, she found her Amulet on the table, laid between two dirty bowls.

Hanna saw her discover it, and touched the Oval defensively. Paragrin raised her eyes.

"I want to know more about this Amulet," said Hanna.

"And I want to know what right you have to take it from me," Paragrin shot back.

"Every right!" said Hanna, coloring. "You come into my colony without warning, stalking my streets like a spy—how was I to know it wasn't *mine?*"

"Yours!"

"Mine! *My* Oval. I wouldn't believe your story now if it wasn't for . . ." Hanna closed her eyes, and her brother came up beside her, putting an arm around her shoulders.

"Where did you find this Amulet?" he asked Paragrin.

"I didn't 'find' it. I'm supposed to wear it," she answered. "It was passed to me officially last year by our Holy Intermediator and our—" She was about to say "Half-Divine" but paused, wondering if she should disclose the information.

"Did your Half-Divine bestow it on you?" said Giles.

Paragrin stared at him. How could he have known? "Yes," she said after a moment. "Jentessa."

Giles nodded and looked across at his sister. Hanna's face was tired and she did not meet Paragrin's eyes.

"You're absolutely sure it isn't yours?" Giles asked her softly. "It's been over fourteen years."

Hanna took up the Oval from the table. "I can't feel my presence here," she said, and when Giles glanced at her, still doubtful, some of her old spirit returned. "I'd know if it was mine, you tangler, don't tell me my way!" She looked back at Paragrin at last. "So you are a ruler of the Melde Colony," she said.

"I told you so hours ago!"

"Where's the Rectangle?" asked Giles.

"Where it should be," replied Paragrin, fighting down her annoyance. "With my mate, in the Melde!"

"That boy at the Wall isn't her mate, Mother, or even her lover," said Meridor. "He's just a friend."

"You found that out soon enough, didn't you?" Hanna glared at her, then turned and, with a tremble in her hands, placed the Oval back around Paragrin's neck. "Release her," she said to the officer, and turned away again.

Meridor jumped up. "Can I go release the other one?" she asked, but Hanna ordered her to sit.

"You attend to this woman," she said, pointing to Paragrin. "Maybe you'll learn something. You already know how to flirt."

Meridor sat and looked at Paragrin with extreme disinterest.

"I don't understand any of this," said Paragrin, as she rubbed the chafes on her wrists. "I didn't even know there was another colony. And if you don't have Amulets, then what happened to them? Are they lost?"

Giles didn't seem interested in answering her question. "I can't imagine," he said instead, "what would take a ruler this far from her duties in her own city. I'll assume you had a good excuse, but whether you did or not, I think that you and your friend should go back home as soon as possible."

"Finding your colony was enough to justify my journey," said Paragrin, disliking his tone. "Why should we turn back again so quickly?"

"Because we have no love for your colony or for your Half-Divine," said Hanna.

Paragrin turned to her.

"Oh, we know all about the Melde," the woman continued, coming to confront her. "We know about its easy ways, its soft people, luxuriating in the good Maker's love. You have had everything, while we at the Vasser have had nothing—not even our Amulets to suggest that we were blessed." Hanna's voice shook, and Paragrin stared back at her, surprised.

"You spoke of blasphemy, my young friend," Hanna muttered, "but how can one blaspheme against a Maker who allows this outrage to continue? Who showers Its favors unevenly? Giving one colony Its blessing with both Its Half-Divine and peace, while condemning the other with Magramid."

Magramid—that name again.

"Who is Magramid?" asked Paragrin.

Hanna smiled at her, as if amazed by her stupidity. "Our loving patron, of course," she said. "Our Half-Divine." When Paragrin still looked confused, Hanna threw out her hands. "Don't you know anything? Did you think Jentessa was the only Half-Divine born of the Maker?"

"No," said Paragrin quickly. "Jentessa said there were ten—

ten who went forth across the world to found a colony . . ."

"A colony?" Hanna let out a laugh. "Your Melde, naturally. As if the Melde were the only one of the ten colonies worth—"

Ten colonies! Paragrin was struck by the number, but she caught herself, flushing. "If I don't know any more, it's because Jentessa didn't think I needed to know," she declared, defensively. "I trust her judgment completely! We have a different view of things in the Melde, you see: we respect the Maker Essai and our Half-Divine. We don't throw their names about so casually."

"Casually!" cried Hanna.

"No more," said Giles. "We're getting nowhere. It's late. Morning's the time for talking." He dismissed the officer and took a blanket from the shelf above the hearth, handing it to Paragrin. "You can wring out your clothes and sleep here by the fire tonight if you want. Maybe it'll burn off your shivers. And Meridor will bring you something to eat from the cellar."

"But, Uncle," said Meridor, rising from her chair, "what about the boy?"

Suddenly the door was flung open and in leapt Kerk with his knife drawn. Hanging from each chained wrist was a splintery chunk of wood that swung as he moved. His eyes were round, his face alert and challenging. With a dangerous smile he danced about, brandishing his knife at his captors.

Paragrin looked across at him, the blanket in her arms, waiting. Kerk glanced from her to the others and then back to her, his feet slowing in their dance until they stopped altogether.

"Well," he said, returning the knife to his belt with a flourish, "it was good of you to tell me we were freed."

"*We?*" said Paragrin, but Meridor seized the other blanket from the shelf and presented it to her new love.

"Welcome," she said, "to the Vasser!"

12

The day after the earthquakes, the weather in the Melde was miraculously beautiful. The springtime temperatures hovered in that perfect middle: warm enough to renounce the winter season forever, and cool enough not to regret its passing already. Birds chorused in the blooming branches and craftspeople found reason to chorus among themselves in the entryways of their shops, abandoning— just for the moment—the work to do within. The planters in the fields remarked about the fragrance of the earth for the first time that spring, and the soil, rich with new shoots of life, seemed particularly receptive to their nursing. It was extraordinarily pleasant, all of it, and did more to comfort the shaken colony than a year of ordinary days could have hoped for. But none of this mattered to Magramid; the important thing was, the Ruler of the Melde was happy.

She knew Cam was happy, for she walked with him all morning as he surveyed the reparations of the city. No one was more cheerful than Cam was, except perhaps Magramid herself, for she was liking his company. The wild man, with a white bandage wound around his head, made one of the company, too, but he was not cheerful. He felt resentful— not toward his attacker, which only his unnatural love could account for—but toward the other, this mortal who had charmed his mother.

"Look at them," said Notts, as the trio paraded by in the court. "Walking together, practically hand-in-hand, when only yesterday that woman tried to murder her son!" He shook his head, his fingers weaving together distractedly.

"Yes, it's a queer thing," said Atanelle, her eyes following the three along. "Very queer."

"Well, the queerest thing of all is that Cam allows this," said Notts.

"That doesn't surprise me," said Atanelle; "you know how he wants to be forgiving."

"Being forgiving is one thing," said Notts.

"—and being stupid is another," Ram concluded.

Notts and Atanelle turned to find the old Ruler beside them, his shrewish eyes squinting at the trio as they disappeared into one of the streets surrounding the city.

"I wasn't going to say—" Notts began indignantly.

"Someone should," said Ram. "That woman's a terror."

"To terrible people, maybe," said Atanelle, and gave Ram a knowing look. He bared his teeth in reply.

"No, it's not as simple as that, unfortunately," said Notts with a sigh. "That son of hers can hardly be called 'terrible.' He's pathetic and loving despite it all, and yet she spurns him. It's a wonder he wasn't killed."

"Well, all I have to say is this, Notts," said Atanelle, drawing herself up, "if Cam believes in her innocence or her softheadedness or whatever, then *I* believe in it, too. It's my duty. And," she said, eyeing her companion, "you might ask yourself if it's your duty, too." She nodded at him pointedly and left, her fat braid swinging out behind her.

"I don't know . . ." mumbled Notts.

"Oh, don't twist yourself up over *her* words," said Ram with a sneer. "She's just in love with Cam, that's all. Talk about pathetic! So naturally she'll go along with anything he says." He lowered his voice. "That's why women should stay out of positions of power, you know," he concluded, patting Notts on the back. "They're far too emotional."

Notts smiled faintly at the grin stretched across Ram's face. "Well!" was all he could reply, and with a quick bow, he hurried off down the court toward his riverside home.

Ram peered after him. "Posy," he muttered.

Cam, Magramid, and the wild man had just entered the street which was lined on both sides with craftshops—and craftspeople who were out enjoying the air just for a moment—when Cam excused himself from Magramid to talk to a particularly pretty young woman who was standing in front of the weaver's house. Before Magramid had time to process the insult, her son had seized the opportunity—and her skirts—to express his dissatisfaction.

"Don't tell me of your sorrows," said Magramid, who, having been on her best behavior all morning in front of Cam, was glad to be able to snap at him. "I never told you to come here. Go back if you don't like it."

"I thought you came to hurt their Rulers," said the half-man. "Now you're helping him. You like him. You like him better than me."

At first Magramid's eyes widened ominously; then the absurdity of it all overtook her rage. "Of course I like him better than you," she said with a laugh. "I even like Jentessa better than you."

A few steps away, the object of their argument put an arm around Ellagette's shoulders. "It's good to see you came through the earthquakes all right," said Cam. "I'm sorry I couldn't come earlier. I promised Kerk that I'd keep an eye on you while he was gone."

Ellagette raised an eyebrow. "He really asked you to do that?"

"Well," said Cam, "no. But it was understood."

Ellagette's mouth curved in that insightful way it had when Kerk's virtues were being discussed. "Thank you, anyway," she said. "When your brother gets back you can tell him that I survived alone." She started back into the shop, then paused in the door frame, debating. "When did you say he was due home?" she asked.

"In a week or so, I hope," Cam replied. "Too long a time for my taste."

Ellagette didn't look at him, but she nodded before she disappeared into the shop, and Cam smiled.

"They are going to get Joined eventually, you know," he remarked, when Magramid came up beside him. "The problem is, they don't know it."

"Who is she?" asked Magramid.

"My brother's mate. Well, not 'mate,' " said Cam. "I have to remind myself they're not Joined—yet." He elaborated as the three of them wound their way toward the riverside, wrongly assuming that they might have an interest in the affair.

"Kerk has some strange idea about what Joining means,"

said Cam. "He thinks he won't have fun anymore. He thinks that taking on any kind of responsibility for another person will be the death of him, the death of his free nature." Cam laughed. "He can't believe that I really enjoy my partnership with Paragrin, despite its problems."

"It has problems?" asked Magramid, her interest rising.

"Every partnership has some problems," said Cam as they passed from the streets onto the riverbank, and he turned, gesturing to the wild man. "You were Joined once to his father. Surely you had some problems."

Magramid was silent. She gazed back at the half-man with a look that Cam mistook for caring, but she was remembering her moment with the father and did not see the son.

Cam watched the emotion play on her old face and, ignorant of the jealous glances the half-man cast upon him, was heartened and took the woman's hand in his to lead her a short distance away.

"I've been thinking, Magramid," he said, "that it would help your relationship with your son if you helped him— helped him to become more civilized."

"Don't you think I've tried?" returned Magramid. "He's beyond help. Look at him."

"But there are things you can do," said Cam. He studied the woman. "I've never heard you call him by name. Does he even have one?"

Magramid shrugged. "He doesn't deserve a name," she said. "He's less than human."

"He's your son!" Cam said, despondent. "Isn't there any bond between you? How can you cast off your own blood so casually?"

Magramid was stung: not by the words, but by the sharp disapproval of Cam's voice. She reached out for his arm. "He does have a name," she said. "When he was a little child, before I knew he was peculiar, I called him Ty, after his father."

"Ty!" Cam smiled. "There. I knew you had loved him once. Now call him. See if he remembers his name."

Magramid moved her gaze warily to the wild man crouched on the ground behind them. He was pulling impatiently at the grass, unaware of their sudden attention.

"Ty," she said.

The wild man paused in his work, his rough hand frozen above the ground.

"Ty," she said again, and the man raised his bandaged head slowly, his eyes round with surprise.

Cam was pleased. "Ask him to come to you," he whispered.

"Come here," said Magramid.

The gratitude in the wild man's face was unmistakable. Cam was much affected and watched breathlessly as the man rose to his feet, his shaggy arms held out toward his mother.

The reunion rushed to its climax: Ty went to embrace her—and just before they were to touch, Magramid turned her back on her son and looked up at Cam.

"Was that right?" she asked.

Cam was speechless with dismay at this final failure. The foolishness of the plan overwhelmed him now, and Cam looked across at Ty apologetically for having made his mother's indifference only more obvious to him. But the wild man accepted no regrets. He shot Cam a violent glare before bolting into the forest surrounding the Melde to hide from his shame.

"I told you he was beyond help," said Magramid, and slipped an arm through Cam's. "At least that got rid of him. Now we can enjoy this beautiful day alone."

The old woman's fingers seemed unusually cold, and Cam put them aside. "No," he said. "I'm sorry. I have matters to see to by myself today."

"I'll come with you," said Magramid, but Cam shook his head.

"No. I said I have to see to them by myself."

He started toward the central court. Magramid, unable to accept the rejection, hurried to get back his arm. Revulsion swept over Cam as the cold hand pressed upon him again.

"I said no!" he declared, and pushed her away. Magramid lost her balance, toppling to the ground, and a second later she lay unconscious on the grass.

"Oh, my Maker!" Cam gasped, and fell to his knees beside her. "Magramid . . ." He stared at her motionless form in disbelief, then scooped the fragile body into his arms. "What have I done?" he moaned, stumbling toward the city. "It's all my fault!"

The Half-Divine lay hugged in his arms, deeply content at last, and pressed her wrinkled face to his chest all the way back to the House.

13

In the Vasser, the morning after the imprisonment bloomed a brilliant shade of blue. At the leaders' house, Paragrin unwrapped herself from the blanket Giles had given her and dressed, going back to the hearth then to see if her boots had dried; they had, and were warm. She drew them on, tucking the bottoms of her trousers into the cuffs.

"Have you had breakfast?"

It was Hanna come at last from her bedroom. Paragrin looked up to meet her eye, and in that quick exchange each gauged the other's mood. Thus warned, Paragrin stood and forced a smile.

"Yes, thank you. Giles made some delicious hot cereal."

Hanna nodded. "And where's your not-mate-not-lover friend?"

"He went back to look at the far-water."

"The ocean?"

"Right; that is what your daughter called it."

Hanna made a face. "She went with him?"

"Believe me," said Paragrin, "he didn't resist her suggestion."

For an instant they shared their annoyance; then Hanna said, "Well!", breaking the moment, and went away to peer into the kettle. Paragrin straightened one of the chairs.

Hanna took a bowl from the mantel, filling it. "Well!" she said again, turning her back on the other, "you'll be leaving today."

Paragrin was silent, then asked in a quiet voice, "Is that a command?"

Hanna took her cereal and circled to the table, keeping her eyes trained on the other. "Do you doubt," she said slowly, "that I have that authority?"

"I have yet to see the evidence," said Paragrin, "and as long as I'm the only one here with proof of leadership, I think I should be the one to make that decision."

"What insolence!" cried Hanna, slamming down her bowl. "How dare you try to usurp me in my own house. I'll have you beaten for such arrogance."

Paragrin's jaw fell. "Then you don't even deserve an Amulet," she said, flushing, "if you can treat my Oval and its sanctity so lightly."

"Lightly? Oh, save me . . ." Hanna dropped into the chair, her hands clapped to her head.

Paragrin trembled. "It was just this sort of irreverence that cost you your Oval, wasn't it?" she charged.

"No!" said Hanna, pressing her temples.

"The Maker took the iron from you!" said Paragrin.

"*Not* the Maker. Magramid."

"Your Half-Divine; that's almost the same as the Maker, isn't it?"

"No!" said Hanna, clenching her hands. "Or if it is, then the world is surely damned."

Paragrin fell silent, watching her. A moment passed; then Hanna, with her face gone as invulnerable as stone, raised her eyes.

"You are distressed," she said softly, the old mockery returned to her voice, "that Giles and I violated your dignity last night—yet you know nothing of real violation! You, a child coddled by the good and true Jentessa."

"I was never 'coddled,'" said Paragrin.

"But were you ever suppressed?" Hanna countered. "Constrained, used, punished for daring to lift your mortal voice against the sacred tyranny? Of course not. And yet we at the Vasser have had to live with this injustice every day."

"I'm having a hard time believing that," said Paragrin. "A Half-Divine would never act so dishonorably. They're like parents, almost: nurturing, caring."

"You know nothing," snapped Hanna, "of the real world."

Paragrin flushed again. "If what you say is true, then why don't you fight this terrible Magramid?" she demanded. "Resist her; refuse to forgive her domination."

"Forgive her? Hardly," said Hanna. "You forget how Half-Divines have magic, how they can control the weather. They can create storms at sea and force whole fishing fleets to shore. They can keep rain away for days, for months! Until every crop is withered dry. How can we resist that," said Hanna, "save with our lives? And believe me, they've been sacrificed often enough."

"Your Half-Divine killed people?"

"Oh, child, you are an innocent," said Hanna, and sat back in her chair. "Of course she killed people. Every uprising against her brought death. Once . . . she brought something even worse."

"Worse than death?" asked Paragrin, uncertain that she wanted to hear what it could be.

"Magramid took a liking to a man once," said Hanna. "It

107

happened a long time ago, when I was Meridor's age, but I remember it clearly. He was a good man, a boat builder named Tyron. He wasn't particularly handsome, but he had a way about him, a gentleness that made him a favorite with everyone—but also with Magramid. I don't know exactly how it happened. It started with her visiting him here in the colony; he was too kind or too frightened to repel her, and really, what could he have done? What can any of us do against a Half-Divine?"

"What . . . did she do to him?" said Paragrin, her eyes widening.

"She raped him," said Hanna, ". . . somehow. It chills the mind to think of it. He killed himself eventually; we were almost grateful—he wasn't the same afterward. And nine months later, she gave birth to that warped and unnatural creature, her son." Hanna shuddered.

Paragrin stared at her, unable to believe, not wanting to believe such a horrifying tale, but there was no mockery in Hanna's voice now. "Sweet Maker," she breathed.

"*Sweet* Maker, indeed!" said Hanna.

"When did she take your Amulets?" asked Paragrin, eager to change the subject.

"Well, it was my fault, really," said Hanna. "I did a foolish thing. I lost my temper after she killed Evan in one of those uprisings. Evan was my mate," she explained, when Paragrin looked at her, "Meridor's father. I suppose I was lucky to have been punished so lightly. If it hadn't been for the sacred law protecting rulers, she most certainly would have killed me. As it was, she merely took my Amulet and Giles's, leaving us to rule without any kind of blessing. We did have them, you see," she said, leveling a look at Paragrin, "for a little while. And when I saw you with an Oval, I thought for a moment that it was mine, that Magramid had found some reason to return it . . . Ah, well."

"But surely," said Paragrin quietly, "the Maker blesses your power even without the Amulets."

"Does It? I don't even care anymore. The Vasser has existed without the Maker's 'love' and has learned to rely on its own good humanity for strength rather than on some negligent deity. And we are made strong by our independence. We've beaten It, you see, just by surviving."

"But you can't blame the Maker for what Magramid has done," protested Paragrin. "After all, It created Jentessa, too; there is good."

"When 'good' Jentessa comes to the Vasser, I'll consider a change of mind," said Hanna, "maybe. Until then, the Maker Essai and I are enemies." She enjoyed Paragrin's affronted expression. "Come, child, look around you!" she said. "Is the Vasser failing? Are my people starving, defeated? We're proud of what we've accomplished in spite of our obstacles. We are a community of one purpose, with hardly any rebellion. Can you say the same about the Melde? So! Without the Maker, who is *never* here, and without Magramid, who is not here at the moment, life is right enough."

Paragrin began a retort, but then a troublesome question occurred to her. "Where exactly is Magramid?" she asked.

Hanna shrugged again. "I don't know. No one's seen her for a week or so. It could be that she's gone back down to the Center. Legend tells us that when a Half-Divine's mortal body grows old, it can be renewed—become young again, so to speak, and Magramid wears a very old body these days. Soon she might return here as a girl! Wouldn't that be exciting? I do hope you'll get to meet her. I'm sure she'd be delighted to meet *you*."

Paragrin drew back.

Hanna leaned forward. "Not frightened, are we?"

Paragrin met her eyes and could not bear the satisfaction playing there. She sat straighter in her chair. "No," she said. "Certainly not."

"Then allow me to recant my command," said the other. "Stay for a week, both you and your not-mate-not-lover friend. See Magramid, perhaps; see how a Makerless colony thrives, definitely! It may change your feelings about your own childish dependence."

"Trusting in the Maker is not a dependence."

"Call it what you will," said Hanna. Her eyes shone.

Paragrin frowned. "All right," she answered at last, "but I won't promise to like it here."

"Well, that reaction would be only fair," said Hanna, "since, without ever seeing it, I already despise the Melde!" She pushed her now-cold bowl of cereal aside and offered a plump hand across the table. "Allies, then, for the moment?"

"Cautious ones, at least," returned Paragrin, and took her hand.

"I'll do what I can to get Mother to let you stay," said Meridor, as she walked back with Kerk into the city. "It's so wonderful to have a new face to talk to! I saw the ocean with a different set of eyes this morning. *Kerk!*"

Meridor stamped her foot. "Why aren't you looking at me while I'm talking? Why are you worrying about that child?"

"I lost sight of him," he said, and stepped out from the flow of traffic to stand against a sailmaker's shop.

"Wasn't that the point?" said the girl. "Didn't you tell him to quit following us? I'm glad you did; he was getting annoying."

"I know, but I feel guilty now." Kerk searched through the crowd behind him with his eyes, thwarted by the shortness of his quarry.

Meridor sighed. She went to stand beside Kerk and, having nothing better to do—what better thing was there?—fell to studying him while he studied the crowd. His face was so sculptured, so perfect—then all at once it contorted. Meridor pulled back in surprise.

"Oh, I was afraid of this!" he said and, without another word, bolted into the crowd.

"Kerk!" called Meridor, but he had forgotten her completely. When she saw the object of her love snatch the little boy up in his arms, she pursed her lips and, flipping her heavy hair behind her shoulders, stalked the rest of the way home, alone.

"You put me down!" shrieked Boon, struggling in Kerk's hold. People passing by in the street turned to stare at them. An officer in conversation with a fish vendor looked up at the noise. "Let me go or I'll say that you're kidnapping me!" cried the boy.

Kerk smiled apologetically at the officer, who frowned before returning to his talk, and put Boon down on his feet.

Kerk kept fast hold of his hand, though, and pulled him aside into an alley.

"What do you think you were doing," Kerk charged, "by trying to steal another fish?"

"What do you care?" said Boon angrily.

Kerk wrapped a fist around the little boy's wrist and shook it. "Do you want this to be cut off?"

"I don't get caught," said Boon, and Kerk narrowed his eyes.

"That was cruel," he muttered. "And besides, it doesn't matter if you don't get caught now, today; you'll get caught someday, and then that's it—maimed for life!"

Boon jerked away. "What do you care?" he said again, and crossed his arms tightly on his chest, glaring at the wall in front of him with a ferocious face.

"Why are you so mad at me?" asked Kerk, squatting down beside him. There were tears threatening to break from Boon's eyes, and Kerk spoke more gently, putting his hand on his shoulder. "Just because I wouldn't talk to you on the beach?"

"You said last night that I had a home by your side," accused Boon, still glaring at the wall.

"Well . . . right," agreed Kerk, remembering those words for the first time. "But that doesn't mean you have to follow me every moment, does it? I'm a young man! A little boy hasn't any steady place with a buck like me."

Just then a father and son passed by, laughing, in the road. The father was not much older than Kerk, the son just a year or so younger than Boon. When Kerk looked back at the boy, Boon shot him a terrible scowl and pushed past him into the street.

"Now, wait!" called Kerk, as he stood up. "You're acting like a child." Boon was disappearing again into the morning crowd. "Oh, bother," said Kerk and, after a moment's debate, went after him.

When he found him again, he grabbed Boon and set him down on the edge of a fish barrel, sending two cats flying to the ground. "Now you listen to me," said Kerk. "I am not your father. I could never be your father. If you want, I'll be your brother—like my big brother is to me. Is that all right?"

The boy pushed at his wet eyes with the heel of his hand. "Does that mean I can be with you?" he asked in a small voice.

Kerk sighed. "Yes!" he said. "Almost always, but sometimes I'll need some privacy and you'll have to respect that. We'll have a secret signal between us. Something like this . . ." Kerk shook his right boot. "Do you understand?"

"Yes," said Boon, and a shy smile broke across his face. "I'm sorry I was mad at you."

"Don't worry about it, but there's one more thing you need to realize—and you may not like it," said Kerk.

"What?" Boon's smile dissolved.

"One day very soon I'll have to go back to my own colony," said Kerk.

"Why? Can't I go with you then?"

"No, you can't." Kerk looked hard at the boy. "You don't belong there." When Boon's eyes started to fill again, Kerk raised an eyebrow. "That's how it has to be," he said. "So you can have me as a big brother for a while, or you can forget me now. It's up to you."

Boon's lip trembled. He studied the crowd, his legs kick-

113

ing the barrel beneath him. "I want to be with you for a while," he said at last, and Kerk grinned.

"Wonderful!" he said. "All right, then. Climb up here." He offered his back, and Boon, his tears forgotten, scrambled up onto his shoulders, delighted.

They marched then—taller than the rest—down the street, together.

14

"*There's absolutely nothing wrong* with this woman," said the Keeper of the House. She stood above the bed in the second chamber, her arms folded decisively beneath her bosom. "You can stop punishing yourself anytime, Cam. You haven't hurt her."

"But she's still unconscious!" he exclaimed, throwing out his arms.

"She's resting," said Aridda.

"I pushed an old woman," moaned Cam, "and now she's dying."

"Oh, mud," said Aridda, losing patience. "I can't believe that you'd push anyone hard enough to bruise them, let alone kill them."

"But this was different," said Cam, sinking down in the chair. "She made me feel so strange."

"Well," said Aridda, giving Notts the eye across the chamber, "she's been provoking a lot of fine emotions lately. Now come away and eat something. You'll feel better."

"I'll be down in a while," said Cam. "I want to be here when she wakes up."

"That old woman will wake up when she wants to wake

up," said Aridda, and passed into the hallway, giving Notts another look as she went.

"Notts." Cam rose from his station by the bed as the little man went toward him. "I did something else terrible, too. I tried to make Magramid acknowledge her son. I thought that maybe if she called him by name, she'd realize how much she loved him."

"Oh, Cam . . ."

"She did love him once," he insisted. "She had to! And I thought . . . I thought that maybe I could make her . . . But I only made matters worse."

"Cam." The Holy Intermediator put a hand up to his shoulder. "I do admire your optimism, your caring, even your great sense of forgiveness; it's what makes you so special above all other leaders the colony has had."

"I know what you're going to say," Cam interrupted. "You're going to say that Magramid isn't worth it." Notts was silent, his head bowed. "Well, I won't accept that," said Cam. "I've seen another side of her, Notts, that you haven't. She *has* tenderness; she's just . . . unsettled, and I'm ashamed that I lost patience with her."

"My dear boy," said Notts, "you mustn't be so hard on yourself."

"Go and find the wild man, will you?" asked Cam. "Take Atanelle, just to be safe. He was so angry with me, I don't know what his mood might be."

"All right, but listen," Notts said. "The time will come when you'll have to give up on this woman. Not to imprison her," he said quickly as Cam opened his mouth to protest, "but to give her up to some people who can really take care of her—her and her son. The Rulers' House is not the place for a madwoman . . . or even an unsettled one."

"I know," said Cam after a moment. "But I guess I feel responsible. If I had made certain everyone had had shelter, maybe she wouldn't be so—"

"Her problem is not her shelter," said Notts, exasperated. "It's much deeper, much darker. Can't you see that?"

Cam looked down at him, stung, and saw how his face had suddenly gone tight with urgency and hate. He could not talk about her with Notts. It seemed he couldn't talk to Notts at all these days.

"Just find the son," said Cam, ending the discussion; and Notts, casting him a look, left without another word.

"Cam . . ."

He spun about, to find Magramid reaching for him.

"Are you all right?" said Cam, taking her hand. "I was so worried. I'm sorry," he said, sitting down beside her. "I never meant to harm you. I hope you know that."

"Of course you didn't," said Magramid, and smiled at him.

What a smile! And Cam knew in that moment that he had been forgiven. Why couldn't the others see this part of her? This fine, grandmotherly way she had, when all one's memories of strangeness and cruelty were washed away by a single smile.

"I forgive you as you forgave me," said Magramid. "Come closer." She drew him to her, resting his head against her bosom. "You just forgot how frail I was, that's all," she said.

"Sometimes you seem so strong," Cam murmured, finding some unexplainable comfort in her gentle embrace, the scent of old-woman skin. What few memories he had of his mother came to him then, filling him with soft contentment. Magramid stroked his hair, weaving her knobby fingers through his locks.

"I wish Paragrin were here," said Cam, his head at rest against her. "She'd understand how I feel about you."

"How do you feel about me?" asked Magramid quietly.

Cam began an answer, then paused. "I don't know how to explain it," he said. "You . . . you confuse me."

"You confuse me, too," said Magramid, and Cam sat up, staring at her.

"Do I?" he said. "In what possible way?"

The Half-Divine stared back at him, and there was a vulnerability in her eyes that softened Cam's heart even more.

"You are amazingly different," Magramid said at last. "I don't think you realize it. In all my life—and I've lived a *very* long life . . ."

Cam smiled.

". . . I've only known one other like you."

"Who was he?"

"My mate," said Magramid. "Ty's father."

Cam was clearly pleased. "Thank you," he said. "You must miss him terribly."

"Sometimes," said Magramid. "Not as much lately."

"I miss my mate," said Cam, sighing. "I've had to pretend in front of everyone that I don't, naturally, so they'll think I'm doing fine without her, and I *am*, it's just that every night I lie in bed thinking of her, wishing she were back already."

"You . . . love her?" asked Magramid in a whisper.

"Oh, yes!" said Cam, surprised. "What a strange question. Didn't you love your mate?"

Magramid thought about it. "I don't know," she said at last. "I wanted him."

"Well, that *can* be the same thing," said Cam slowly. A bit of the old discomfort crept back to him as he watched her troubled face brood upon the distinction. He patted her hand and stood up. "Let me bring you some food," he suggested. "Aridda's made a pot of stew downstairs. I'll have some brought up to you, all right?"

"All right," said Magramid, but her mind wasn't on the question. Cam left and went down to the larder to make arrangements.

Magramid lay alone in the shadowy chamber, her hands slowly clenching the blanket.

"Feeling better?" came a voice.

Magramid didn't even look up. Jentessa, with the hood of her cloak back in the privacy of the chamber, went to the foot of the bed.

"You've been puzzling me," she admitted, her sharp eyes upon the other. "I haven't known your plan; you changed it on me without telling, but now I think I'm beginning to understand. You're going to try to seduce him, aren't you?"

Magramid didn't answer.

"You're going to try to seduce him, and destroy his power that way," said Jentessa.

"I'm not trying to destroy him . . . anymore," returned Magramid hotly. "You understand nothing! He has a good, accepting spirit, better than anyone's—better than yours."

"So I'm to believe you're impressed at last!" Jentessa laughed. "Well, you won't succeed by this device either, Magramid. You heard how he loves Paragrin; you haven't a chance." Jentessa moved closer. "Why don't you just go back to the Vasser?" she said. "You've failed here. And as long as Paragrin lives, you'll never win a moment of Cam's real attention." Jentessa gazed at her sister with satisfaction and, without another word, faded down.

Alone in the room, Magramid stared off into space. "As long as Paragrin lives," she echoed, and was silent again.

15

Paragrin waited all the next day to be introduced formally to the Vasser colonists. No ceremony presented itself. And yet she knew the word of her coming had spread; people looked at her differently now and whispered behind their hands, but no one ever bowed to her or allowed her to pass in front of them on the street. In short, there was a strange notion of equality in the Vasser that felt altogether wrong.

"It's honor enough that you're not made to work," said Hanna when Paragrin had come to her with the grievance. "Don't expect these people to treat you like their better. There is no better here."

"You're a 'better,'" said Paragrin.

"Not at all," declared Hanna. "I have a job to do, just like everyone else; no less born to my trade than the sons of the sailmaker. Tell me, friend," she said with a smile, "what sort of house does an Amulet claim in your city? Is it large? Glorious? Set apart from the rest with grand tapestries and carven wood?"

Paragrin laughed at the accuracy. "At least there's never any confusion over who's in charge," she replied.

"There's no confusion here, either," returned Hanna. "It's Magramid."

Magramid. That infamous, unfathomable disciple of the Maker Essai haunted Paragrin on each step of her exploration through the colony. She imagined the unholy daughter having ascended before her in every old woman's face. No! in every *girl's* . . . Any moment she expected to be set upon, but she was too embarrassed to confess this to her hosts.

For it was amazing to her how easily the colonists accepted this way of life, living under the unending threat of Magramid. And yet they did, going on with their tradeswork and fishing just as if nothing horrific had ever happened. The Vasser was strong despite it all, maybe stronger than the Melde in some ways, but Paragrin had trouble seeing it as "thriving," which had been Hanna's description. "Thriving" suggested a certain joy to the work, and there seemed to be little joy here. Everyone was a bit too careful, too guarded, afraid almost to let their spirits shout lest Magramid should hear, and come.

This was why Paragrin decided that the Vasser had missed more than it had gained. What made this colony so strong was a united drive for survival—not a sense of growth, as in the Melde. There was no progression here, as much as there was protection. And this single-minded purpose influenced everything they did.

It simplified their way of living, their sense of right and wrong. There was no real forgiveness in the Vasser, and little room for the foibles of a more natural people. For all Hanna's claims to humanity over devotion, in the end it was the Melde that seemed more humane. And yet, thought Paragrin, if her colony had had Magramid to contend with instead of Jentessa, would it have turned out so differently? Her soul ached, for the first time since she left, for the familiar customs of home—and for the open and trusting heart of her Cam. There was none of his kind to be found anywhere here. And that, too, thought Paragrin with a sigh, was what was missing.

Kerk and Boon were walking side by side through the city. The fishing boats had just returned on a late-afternoon tide and the streets were swarming with people.

"Why do girls look at you so much?" Boon demanded, "and with such stupid expressions?"

Kerk laughed, swinging his catchbag of clams into his other hand.

"Oh, that's it, is it?" said Boon. "They think that you're fine?"

"I suppose so," said Kerk.

Boon nodded. "I thought maybe you had seaweed on your head or something."

Kerk dove for the boy and scooped him, squealing, into his arms. "You're a rascal," he said, and turned him upside down. Boon shrieked, then giggled as his shirt slid down around his chest.

They traveled in this unconventional way until Kerk suddenly set the boy on his feet again and took firm hold of his hand.

"Why did you put me down?" Boon complained, pulling on his arm. "I liked hanging wrong-ways."

"People were frowning at us," said Kerk, marching him forward.

"Who cares?"

"You should," Kerk returned. "You have to act responsibly, Boon, or you'll never amount to anything."

The boy stared up at him, bewildered.

"I'm just telling you for your own good," Kerk instructed. "Now you pay mind to what I say."

"All right," said Boon. "But meantime, can you tell me more about your adventures in the world?"

"Of course," said Kerk, greatly pleased, "as long as you understand that I was forced into these situations, and never went off seeking them myself. That would have been irresponsible on my part, you understand."

"I understand," said Boon wearily. "I wish you'd just go on with the stories."

"As long as you understand," said Kerk, and launched into his most lawless escapade.

The two of them continued on down the street, so engrossed in the tale that it startled them both when all at once a voice called, "Kerk!"

The two adventurers looked up. That voice belonged to Meridor, who, after casting a quick scowl on the boy, settled her smile on the man.

Boon wrinkled his nose. He had never seen her so ugly. Her hair was down, her skirts were too short, and the lacing was lost from her blouse, practically revealing her top. But the worst thing of all, Boon thought, was the smell of dead flowers that hung about her. He rolled his eyes and pulled on Kerk's sleeve to follow him.

Kerk didn't move. He had never seen Meridor so beautiful, so alluring, with her long hair loose around her shoulders, her legs exposed—and her blouse! Kerk stared down at the absence of the lacing, and a feeling swelled within him that he hadn't felt in days.

"I thought," said Meridor, greatly heartened by this admiring look, "that perhaps you and I could go down and look at the ocean again . . . or something."

Kerk met her eyes. He kept his gaze on her while he pushed back at Boon with the catchbag.

"What?" demanded Boon, warding off the clams.

"Take these," said Kerk through his teeth.

"Why?"

Kerk turned on him. "Because I want to be alone with her now. Remember? That was part of our deal."

Boon looked up at Meridor, who was smiling triumphantly, and he frowned. "You didn't give me the secret signal," he said.

"Oh, rot," said Kerk, and shook his boot. "There!"

"When am I going to hear the rest of the story?" asked Boon, taking the clams. "I want to know what happens to you and Ellagette."

Kerk stared at the boy, his frustration caught upon his face.

"I suppose it has a responsible ending," sighed Boon.

"Kerk . . ." said Meridor, suddenly uncertain of her claim, "must you spend every minute with this child?"

Kerk still stared at Boon, fighting for an answer, when a waft of perfume—aided in its progress by Meridor—drifted to his nose. He turned to her. "Of course not," he said.

"It doesn't have a responsible ending?" piped Boon, clapping his hands.

"Of course it does!" Kerk said, spinning back to him. "Now go away. I can't spend all my time with children, can I?"

Boon hunched his shoulders against the sting. "Who's asking you to?" he said. "I don't care!" And he ran off into the crowd, the catchbag of clams bouncing against his back.

Meridor narrowed her eyes as Kerk watched him go, and deciding not to leave another opportunity to chance when she had come this far, she seized Kerk's hand and pulled him into the shadows between two buildings to press her advantage—and her lips—against his.

"Responsibility," Kerk murmured, but then the feeling swelled within him again, and he returned her kisses, harder.

16

Magramid had stayed in her bed for two days thinking over her situation. Jentessa was right: it had changed. *She* had changed somehow. She couldn't explain it, any more than she could have explained what had happened before, all those years ago, with the other one. All she knew was that she wanted Cam. That was really not the problem. The problem was, she also wanted him to want her, and therein lay the difficulty. There was a rival.

And not an ordinary rival. Not a paltry everyday kind of woman she could crush without thinking. This one was a ruler, and Magramid was too aware, still, of the Maker's law protecting rulers. So another path to his desire had to be found. And after hours of brooding and a moment of inspiration, the solution to her problem presented itself to Magramid in all its wonderful simplicity, and she called for the wild man to come and to hear her.

Ty hadn't been in the House long. He had eluded the search yesterday by Notts and Atanelle, and only just returned at sundown to seek comfort by his mother's side. He had forgiven her—naturally—but his hatred for Cam had deepened. Magramid knew this, and using his desire for vengeance as a lure, she drew the half-man into her plan.

She told him how it would work. She told him how Cam would suffer; and when she unfastened her bodice to reveal the two stolen Amulets that hung around her neck, Ty took the Oval eagerly and hid it in his hand until everything was ready.

And then they went down the stairs together.

Cam was sitting in the dining room before a fatlamp, caught in the crossfire between the cutting words of his grandfather and Atanelle. His head rested wearily on his hand as the dispute raged around him.

"If your Ruler says that you can't go back to the upper chamber, then you can't go!" shouted Atanelle. "You're lucky to stay here at all."

"Why don't you let him speak for himself, instead of always butting in with your mouth?" said Ram. "You're not going to let her bully you, are you, boy?"

"Grandfather . . . you knew your use of that chamber was only temporary."

"Yes! But until Paragrin got back, not some queer old woman with her idiot—" Ram stopped, suddenly aware of the two visitors in the entryway. Cam looked up as his grandfather stepped quickly behind him, and Magramid moved into the room, leaning on her son's arm.

"I'm delighted you're well enough to come down," Cam said to her, rising. "Would you like anything to eat? Aridda's gone to bed, but I'm generally considered as good a cook as she."

"Better," said Atanelle. "Much better."

"Or even better, by some," said Cam with a smile. "I'd be happy to—"

"No," said Magramid, taking the chair opposite him. "Thank you, but I would not have quit my bed this evening unless I had a very serious reason to do so. Sit down, child."

Cam stared at her, then at Atanelle, who looked at him with raised eyebrows. "Is something wrong?" he asked.

"I'm afraid so. Sit down."

This time Cam obeyed, his heart beating a little faster than usual. "Is it your health?" he asked quietly. "Have I done more damage than we supposed?"

Magramid gave a little laugh. "Isn't that like you," she said. "Always worrying about some other person's sorrows before your own."

Atanelle, moving Ram out of the way, took a station behind her Ruler's chair. She didn't like the sound of this, and trained her eyes aggressively on the others. Uncomfortable with the new company, Ram removed himself from the shadowy room, hovering just out of sight in the entrance hall to listen. Like two opponents with their seconds, then, Magramid and Cam faced each other across the table, the fatlamp casting a warning glow on the scene.

"I have something terrible to tell you," said Magramid, looking into Cam's earnest eyes, "and you'll need to brace yourself."

"Why don't you just get to the point?" said Atanelle, her hand going protectively to Cam's shoulder.

Magramid dismissed her with a glance and returned her gaze to Cam. This would hurt him, she knew, but it was necessary. If his sorrow softened her resolve, she would remind herself of that. She must.

She took a breath. "We were wondering where my son had gone to," she said. "When he came back today, he told me. He had been down along the river, hours and hours away."

Cam's anxiety was checked. He hesitated. "Did you think that was bad of him?" he asked. "Is this all you're talking about?"

Magramid shook her head. "Ty saw something when he was there. Something terrible."

"*What?*" the warrior demanded. "Why don't you say it?"

"Atanelle . . ." Cam hushed her and glanced up at Ty. The wild man wore a look of victory on his unshaven face, of hatred satisfied; and Cam did not trust his smile. He turned back to Magramid and for a moment wondered at her own sincerity, but only for a moment. She stifled her appetite, and Cam saw the grandmother again.

"What did Ty see?" he asked.

Magramid prepared herself. "He saw a crude wooden raft broken against the rocks," she said, "with two broken bodies strewn across it—a young woman's and a young man's . . . a man who might have been handsome before, with dark wavy hair.

"He didn't know who they were at first," continued Magramid. "His mind is so simple, all he thought was that the woman's face seemed familiar, but then he remembered. He had seen her here before, just outside the House."

Cam's eyes widened. Atanelle's hand tightened on his shoulder.

"They were dead," said Magramid, "and had been, it seems, for days. Think carefully . . . which two people have been gone now for days?"

Cam stared at her. "What are you hinting at?" he said suddenly. "That it was Paragrin? and . . . and my brother? They weren't traveling by raft, so forget that thought. They would have no business on a raft." He stood up. "It must have been other people. We'll have to find out who. Ask around, Atanelle, to see if—"

"I thought your brother was an adventurer," interrupted Magramid, her eyes like chains then, upon him. "And your mate certainly was! Why couldn't she have constructed a raft? Why couldn't she have ridden it, have lost control—"

"No!" said Cam, slamming his fist on the table. "It wasn't her. She's far too responsi—far too good a traveler," he concluded. "Why are you scaring me like this? I won't hear of it!"

Magramid's heart ached to see the terror on his face. She reached for his hand, pleading with him. "Do you think I would put you through this if I didn't have to?" she said. "It pains me to see you this way! But it is necessary for you to hear this. It is *necessary*." She pulled his hand toward her. It was shaking, and she turned it over so that his palm was exposed. "Ty," she commanded, "give him what you took from the dead girl."

The joke revealed at last, Ty slapped the Oval down to Cam's hand.

He leapt back as if the iron had seared him. The Amulet dropped, rattling for an instant on the table, then lying still. Lifeless. From the entryway, Ram's eyes bulged.

"No!" cried Cam. His face drained completely of color. "They can't be dead! Maybe they're still alive. Take me to them," he said, turning to Ty. "Maybe they're—"

"They were dead!" insisted Magramid. "Ty pushed them back into the water and they floated away with the current."

"Great Maker!" Cam said to him, his face contorting. "You drowned them!"

The wild man returned a little smile, and Cam was on him in an instant, shaking him.

"You killed them!" he cried.

The humor gone, Ty struck Cam away, sending him to the floor. The next second Atanelle had thrown Ty down.

"Strike him again and you're dead!" she shouted.

Ty rose to combat her, but Magramid stopped him.

Atanelle went to help Cam. When she pulled him to his feet, he leaned heavily against her, trembling in her arms.

"They can't be dead," he whispered. "Not *both* of them . . ."

"I'm taking you upstairs," she told him. "We'll talk there. It'll be all right."

"Let me help!" said Magramid, reaching for Cam's hand.

"Haven't you helped enough?" barked Atanelle, and hustled Cam past her into the entrance hall, where Ram drew back, horrified. Atanelle saw him and her face grew more terrible than before. "You keep quiet about this, do you understand?" she said fiercely. "Not a word about their deaths until he decides what to do."

"Yes, yes!" squeaked Ram. "I promise."

"Go wake Aridda!" she said, pushing Cam upstairs. "And find Notts. I'm going to need help!"

Ram was off like an arrow, and Magramid and Ty stood alone in the dining room.

But then, not quite alone.

"I can't believe you did that," said Jentessa, staring at her sister in amazement.

"Get away!" cried Magramid. "You have nothing to do with this." She ran up the steps after Cam, and Jentessa followed her to the bottom of the stairs.

She could feel Cam shaking in the room above her. She could sense his quick, uneven breathing, his pain.

"This is absurd," she told herself, a desperate plan! Surely her sister realized she could appear to Cam at any moment, expose it all and ruin her handiwork.

Jentessa closed her eyes, reaching soothingly toward him with her soul. She would tell him with her inner voice that all was well.

Then she stopped herself, her eyes opening. It was too unlike Magramid to be this careless. Something was wrong. Magramid was leaving herself open—becoming practically . . . vulnerable.

Jentessa stared into the upper hallway, where her sister had disappeared, and suddenly she felt something she hadn't known with her: power. Always in their confrontations it had been she who'd been angry, emotional, while Magramid stood coolly by, steady and detached. Magramid had known there was nothing Jentessa could really do to stop her before, not without the Maker's help. Now maybe the time had come. Maybe there was something she could finally do to put an end to Magramid's tyranny. What it would be Jentessa didn't know. Her heart raced with possibilities. It would all depend on Magramid's game.

She stepped back; Cam's suffering slipped from her consciousness. For now—nothing! She would do nothing to save her sister from her own insanity. Let it play, Jentessa told herself, her eyes gone bright and eager, let it play . . . and until the time when she saw her own hand, she would watch, just watch.

And wait.

17

Paragrin sat alone by the fireside the next morning and chewed her lip disapprovingly. Kerk had not come back last night. She might have worried for his safety if his catchbag of clams hadn't arrived in his stead, with a hurried and somewhat petulant explanation from that boy who was the latest of Kerk's disciples. "Gone with the girl" was all Boon had said, and Paragrin was left with the whole night to brood upon his infidelities. Not that Ellagette was such a great friend of hers that Paragrin should feel personally betrayed. But Ellagette was, after all, a woman like herself, and Paragrin felt her female indignation rise up in her defense, regardless.

Besides, it annoyed Paragrin how easily Kerk attracted lovers.

She was just musing on this last point when Giles stumbled sleepily into the kitchen room.

"Hello," she said.

He mumbled a reply and moved past her to the door. What there was of his hair was in wild disarray, the clay-red curls around the back of his head pushing out in all directions. It wasn't surprising, thought Paragrin critically, that no one had wanted to face *that* every morning. Giles, she had learned, had never been Joined.

Ignorant of the judgment he was inspiring, Giles opened the door to let in his friend. This was a morning ritual, and with renewed hope Paragrin held out a hand to the visitor; but the big cat ambled past her without so much as a nod, and went and sat down on the blanket which was still spread at the hearth.

"That animal doesn't like anyone but you," said Paragrin crossly.

Giles chuckled and lit the fire beneath the kettle. The cat stretched its bulk and sat up again, blinking at the brightness of the flame. "My Fidd," said Giles, rubbing his calloused hand along her fur; "she's the best old girl in the world."

He stirred a mixture of wheat and water in the kettle, then turned to widen his eyes playfully at the cat. He lifted a tiny fish from a box at the corner of the mantel and wriggled it above her nose. Fidd sat up on her haunches to sniff it, then took it neatly between her speckled jaws to eat upon the hearth.

Paragrin moved the blanket away and refolded it, watching with wary fascination as the fish was devoured. It was almost as interesting to watch Giles, for he was never so animated during the rest of the day.

"I'm surprised you allow yourself to feed her," said Paragrin with a smile. "What sort of example are you setting for the proud people of the Vasser, letting this cat get fed for nothing?"

Giles peered at her. "You don't know my Fidd," he said, "or you wouldn't insult her so. She's the house warrior, on duty constantly to make certain no mice get past our door. The fish," he said, as he wiped the remnants up with a pot-cloth, "is merely her compensation."

"I should have guessed," said Paragrin, gazing down at her. There was something about the big cat's unlikely silhouette, the broadness of her shoulders, her swagger as she crossed again to the door, that kept reminding her of someone.

Just as Giles was closing the door after her, it opened again and in walked the little boy and Kerk. Kerk was in the best of spirits—Paragrin had known this mood before—and he gave her a special grin before he turned and held a sack out to Giles.

"This is grain!" he said. "I bought it for you myself with the trade of a few choice snails—the least I could do in return for all your kindness."

Giles looked from the boy to him, surprised. "That's very good of you," he said.

Kerk bowed and turned back to Paragrin. "I have something to tell you!" he whispered.

"What makes you think you have to tell me?" she said. "You're the most predictable person I know."

Kerk frowned, and Giles excused himself to go to store the grain in the cellar. Paragrin shot Kerk a knowing look and went to stir the cereal.

"I see you've taken an apprentice to your trade," she remarked, nodding to Boon. "How long will it be before he advances from clam delivery to the actual act?" She turned and made a thoughtful expression. "Weren't you his age when you first—"

"Paragrin!" said Kerk, flushing. "Stop it. You don't know what you're talking about."

"Oh, come now," she said. "You're not going to pretend to be virtuous after all this time, are you?"

"What does 'virtuous' mean?" asked Boon, pulling on Kerk's sleeve.

"Nothing," said Kerk, and glared at Paragrin.

She smiled. "To you, nothing. To Ellagette . . ."

"Boon, wait outside," said Kerk. He said it in that grown-up voice and the boy didn't question it.

When the door closed behind him, Kerk grabbed Paragrin by the wrist. "Don't say those sorts of things in front of the child," he said.

"You might have thought of him before you went off with Meridor," she said. "Now let me go."

Kerk's lip trembled, but he released her. "It's none of your rotten business," he said, "what I do. But I'll tell you my habits just this once. I did not sleep with Meridor."

Paragrin made a face. "The boy himself told me about it, Kerk. You went off with her."

"My Maker, what do you expect?" he cried. "I thought I owed Boon an explanation, but you ought to understand about lust! I know you do . . . It hasn't been so many years ago that that yearning was directed at me."

Paragrin turned, blushing, to the kettle. "I wasn't involved with Cam then," she said. "It's not the same as what you're doing to Ellagette. Besides, we never—"

"And I 'never' with Meridor," said Kerk flatly, "because of Ellagette."

"Since when has that stopped you?"

"Since—since I started thinking," said Kerk.

Paragrin stared at him. She had never seen him so serious, so lost in his own great meditations. It made her want to laugh.

"I think," said Kerk, "that it's easy to be virtuous if your sights never stray. What's hard—what's admirable—is being true in spite of that."

Paragrin felt a comment coming, but she held her tongue.

"For the first time in my life," said Kerk, his eyes shining, "I didn't do something that I really wanted to do. Meridor was determined for me. She was using all the good moves you women try. You can't begin to appreciate how hard it was for me to refuse her. I couldn't even explain it to myself! But all night I was out on the beach, walking around and thinking about my rightful duty to Ellagette—and to Boon."

"And to Boon?" said Paragrin.

Kerk nodded. "I'm his big brother, you know, for now, and the responsibility of it all, of shaping his little views and morals—I had no idea! Suddenly I can understand why Cam was after me all the time to behave. Cam had to be my parents, too, as well as my brother, just as I am to Boon." Kerk shook his head. "I had no idea."

"It's remarkable you came out as well as you did," returned Paragrin.

Kerk narrowed his eyes, then gave her a sad smile. "You'll never give me credit for anything," he said, "but I don't care. Boon respects me. And Ellagette . . . Ellagette will be very proud."

Behind him the door opened a crack. "Can I come in now?" asked Boon, peering in.

Just then Meridor emerged from the back of the house.

Paragrin looked from Boon to her and then back again to Kerk. The selfless hero bowed gallantly to Meridor, whose careful grooming of the day before was reduced now to snarls and rumples, and taking Boon firmly by the hand, he left the two young women standing alone in the kitchen room.

Paragrin blinked.

Meridor scowled. "He makes me crazy," she muttered, and went back to her bed.

18

The curtains in the dining-room windows were drawn, turning back the sun; a tapestry, fastened over the portal, guarded against an unwanted entrance; and so in this private dimness sat the harrowed Ruler of the Melde and his council of mourners. Notts was there, and Atanelle, with Magramid sitting off by herself near the fireplace. All eyes but hers were lifted toward the woman whose pretty face was scored with tears. Magramid did not care, this pain being only a side issue of no particular importance.

Ellagette trembled, staring down at the cold iron Oval that lay upon the table.

Cam reached for her silently, but she let him hold her only for a minute; in the next she pulled away and ran from the room. The tapestry swung back into place and Cam lowered his eyes, gazing at nothing.

Atanelle sucked in her lip and looked across at him. It was frightening, she thought, what tragedy could do to a face in one day. She had never seen him so white. He seemed old, resigned; the terror of last night sapped away, leaving only the inner scars and a faint, shocked look to his eyes. There was a cut, too, on his lip where Ty had struck him. She hated Ty now, despite what she had said to Notts. There would be no forgiving. She had refused to let him into this council, had *wanted* to refuse Magramid, but Cam had risen from his stupor just enough to protest it. Why, Atanelle couldn't imagine, but she hadn't wanted to challenge him. Not on this, of all mornings. She forced her gaze away from Magramid and inspected a crack in the table's polish.

"My Ruler," said Notts gently, "have we reached a decision, then? Are we to keep this terrible news from the people until a suitable replacement can be found?"

Cam played with the Amulet's chain, mindlessly weaving it between his fingers. "Whatever you think is best," he said.

"I think it would be best," replied Notts, "although I can't imagine anyone who could wear this Amulet with as much grace and honor as Paragrin."

"Well," said Cam, starting up, "someone must. I'll spend the rest of my life as a widower, but I can't rule by myself, can I? That wouldn't be right. The Maker's plan is to have a man and a woman lead together. You know that, Notts."

"Yes, my Ruler."

"Here," said Cam, dropping the Amulet into his hands. "You take it. Hold on to it until you can find another woman. I suppose you had better do that soon."

"Yes, my Ruler."

"Where are you going?" asked Atanelle, as Cam stood apart from the table.

Cam seemed caught by the question. "I don't know," he said. "Do I have to report everything I do to you?"

Atanelle's eyes widened. "No, my Ruler. I didn't mean—"

"It sounded as if you meant that," Cam said and frowned,

maneuvering his way awkwardly toward the entrance hall. "You're not in charge here, Atanelle, and if you have any ideas about becoming Ruler, well, you can just forget them. I won't have you!" Cam glared at her, ignoring the wounded look on her face, and escaped past the tapestry into the hall. His steps beat against the stairs, and Magramid slipped out after him.

"My dear friend," said Notts, putting a hand on Atanelle's shoulder, "try not to let it hurt you."

"I know very well that I could never replace Paragrin," said Atanelle, pushing back a tear, "in her rule, or in his heart."

"He didn't mean what he said," Notts assured her. "We must all be patient with him now. He's in such pain."

"I know," said Atanelle. "I just wish there was something I could do." She rose unsteadily from her chair. "I'm going to the tavern, Notts. Is there anything I can bring you?"

He shook his head. "Nothing, thank you. Remember! Not a word . . ."

She nodded and was gone. The Holy Intermediator sank down, miserable, in his chair and gazed at the Oval. How many times had he admired this around dear Paragrin's neck? He felt he knew the Amulet almost as well as she had. Wasn't it ironic, he thought sadly, now that she was dead, that it seemed, somehow, different?

"Come to me," said Magramid.

Cam sat on the corner of his bed, an old nightdress of Paragrin's held in his hand. Magramid had come upon him uninvited, but he did not order her to leave. The sound of her old voice held sweet comfort to his aching soul, and he looked around. Her arms were stretched toward him, and without thinking why, or if he shouldn't, he went to her, letting her wrap her arms around him, letting himself relieve his sorrow in her embrace.

"I will take care of you," she said, and he wept as she stroked his hair. "You'll get over her," she whispered. "You'll have another love, and soon."

"No," said Cam.

"Trust me," said Magramid.

"No!" said Cam louder, and he pulled away. "How can you even say such a thing? I will never find anyone like her again. I will never love again!" He turned indignantly, dragging at his reddened face with his sleeve. "I'm sorry. I know you're just trying to help, Magramid, but you have to understand: I don't *want* anyone but Paragrin. I could no more seek another love than I could another brother. Those are gifts that come but once. No one can replace her; alive or dead, she will always have my heart."

He moved past her toward the door. "I'm going to find Atanelle," he muttered, pushing aside the deer pelt. "I have another apology to make."

When he was gone, Magramid stood alone, stunned to silence by his hateful words. Then her face twisted and she seized upon Paragrin's nightdress, consuming it in flames, the blackened tatters of cloth swirling crazily to the floor.

From afar, Jentessa sensed this all, and a new, terrible, wonderful thought blossomed before her. If Paragrin had actually been *in* that garment—already Magramid would be damned! *This* was the answer! Then the realization of her own depravity swept over her, and Jentessa was ashamed. Nothing was worth the sacrifice of Paragrin's life; she would not allow herself to think it.

But Magramid's madness was temptingly ripe, and try as she might, Jentessa could not put the solution from her mind.

That afternoon, the glorious weather at the Melde ended. No more hovering in that perfect middle, no more birds chorusing in the branches; they screamed, rather, as the storm to end all storms crashed down upon the city. It had come suddenly, clouds lurching across the sky that afternoon, and now people could do nothing but look helplessly out at the rain and the yellow lightning that crackled through the gray. Three trees around the court had already been struck, and their blackened limbs lay dead and shattered on the beaten grass.

The water drummed on Notts's roof. A piece of wood around his chimney had given way, and now a pool of water widened around his hearth, dancing with every new drop the way the river danced close outside his door. The river was rising, but Notts paid no heed to the water in or out of his home; he was too engrossed by his confusion.

The Oval Amulet lay before him on the table, its iron glinting slightly in the glow of a fatlamp.

He did not understand it, but he could not dismiss it. There was something disturbing about the Amulet. For the hundredth time he took it in his hand, squeezing it, feeling the power within the iron. The force of the Maker was there, he couldn't deny that. Why, then, did it feel so *wrong?*

He tried once more to separate the nagging images that swam about in his head, images of Paragrin wearing it, of touching the Oval himself when she had allowed him to study its wonder. Generations old and passed from hand to hand, the Amulet had a great many marks distinguishing its surface. "And every one of them is special," Paragrin had told him when he had offered to file down a jagged notch that had twice cut her hand; "it would be as if you were deleting a part of history." Notts sighed and rubbed his thumb along its edges.

Something.

Something, and he rubbed his thumb along it again. He sat up, pushing the Oval closer to the light. He peered at its surface, turning it over and over in his hand, stroking it.

"Sweet Maker," he gasped. "The notch is gone!"

It was not possible, yet there it was in front of him, as irregular as before, yet smooth. Notts stared at the Amulet in disbelief; pressed in his thumbs and examined it again, yet there was no denying the change. A notch could be cut, it could even be flattened down, but it could not be made to disappear. Not ever.

"My Maker," he said. "It's not hers."

Not hers. *Real*, but not hers. The implication of that made his brain spin as a thousand possible explanations, each more impossible than the next, crowded in upon him; and then he started up from the chair, breathless, for suddenly the most amazing revelation of all burst upon him. If the Oval wasn't Paragrin's, then it wasn't any proof of her drowning.

She wasn't dead. And neither was Kerk.

For half of one moment Notts stood in the middle of the room. By the next half, the Amulet was in his hand and he was running out into the storm.

Below him the river surged between its weakening banks, breaking against and over the rocks in its path: rising, splashing up onto the grass and the mud. Notts struggled on his way, slipping on the treacherous ground to almost lose his proof in the puddles before he thrust the Amulet deep in his tunic and freed his hands to grasp at the branches, the door latches, anything to keep him from falling. There had never been such weather as this.

At last the rank of riverside dwellings fell behind him. He was at the entrance to the court, the watery image of the Great House shimmering in the distance. Notts pushed himself faster, and his ankle slammed against something and twisted, pitching him forward into the mud.

He lay there, stunned, then turned his face into the rain to see what had caused him to trip. But it wasn't a "what" at all: it was Ty.

Notts was startled. He reached up to Ty for help—surely it had been an accident—but then he saw Magramid watching him, studying him through the hammering rain with her too-bright eyes. At first he felt terrified, helpless; then, looking back at those eyes, Notts realized all his feelings of dread about her had had reason. It was she who had brought all these confusions to the city! It was she who had told Cam that his loved ones were dead; and she knew, she *knew*, that they weren't. Somehow, some impossible way, she knew everything.

His righteous fury flared, and Notts struggled to his feet

in spite of his pain, in the midst of the storm, to confront her.

"You're a monster!" he said. "A damnable liar!"

Her expression hardened.

Ram, who had been hurrying from the tavern with two flasks of ale beneath his cloak, slipped headlong into the mud when he heard the sudden cry. Cursing and muttering, he reached through the wet to regain his flasks, when he turned to scowl at the idiots in the storm and froze instead in terrible fascination at the scene.

There was that fool Intermediator, hopping about on one foot and waving his arms at Magramid, that old serpent who had stolen his room—and there was her idiot son! Ram bared his teeth at them. Three imbeciles having a meeting in a storm! He would have dismissed the lot in a minute, and run home to comfort and drink, if there hadn't been something seductively suspicious in the way that the big man was approaching the little one. Ram wiped the rain from his face and stared, shielding the ale flasks and his eyes with the cloak.

Notts and Magramid were having words, obviously. Ram couldn't make out what they were saying, but Notts kept pointing at her, gesturing with his arms. She stood motionless, but he was moving—Ty was moving, slowly, behind Notts. Ram bit his lip with suspense. Notts was obviously too taken with his declamations to notice Ty's approach; he threw out his arms again. One shout Ram heard above the others:

"Paragrin is ali—"

And before Notts could finish, Ty seized him. Ram

squeaked, clapping a hand to his mouth as Notts tried to pull away, but the little man's foot kept buckling beneath him. He was helpless. Ram watched, mesmerized, as the large man lifted up the small one by the neck. Notts gasped, clawing at his captor, but Ty's hold was firm, and beneath the clinging of his shirt the great muscles of the wild man flexed—and then compressed. The Intermediator flailed, snapped, and hung lifeless in his grasp. With a nod from Magramid, Ty flung the man into the turbulence of the river's course.

Ram's mouth fell. "Oh, my stars!" he said.

And then Magramid turned and saw him.

Her secret safe, the Half-Divine's mind was free to listen to the outer world. She had sensed Ram then, in the same way she had sensed Notts before. And now, her plot in jeopardy again, she motioned for Ty to get him.

Ram screamed and left his flasks behind him as he started up, throwing off his cloak and running toward the Great House. He didn't look behind him; he didn't dare. But the wild man was upon him before he was there, the massive hands wrapping around his throat.

"What's all the yelling?"

Atanelle was at the entrance to the House. She wouldn't have been close enough to prevent the murder, but she would have seen who had done it. Magramid pushed Ty aside and drew Ram to her.

"If you breathe a word of what you saw," she said, "you will never breathe another. Do you understand me?"

Shaking violently in her hold, Ram nodded, his pale-blue eyes bulging in their sockets.

She released him and he flew into the House, nearly knocking Atanelle over in the process. She stared at him, then back out at the others. She watched them watching her and wondered distrustfully what possible reason they would have to be there, standing in the midst of a storm. Magramid's eyes flashed out from the rain and Atanelle's narrowed; then the warrior turned on her heel and went back inside, shaking the water from her braid.

"You will have to guard the old man," said Magramid, looking up at her son, "and make certain he doesn't tell."

"I did well today, didn't I, Mother?" asked Ty, grinning down at her. "I killed one man. I can kill another."

"We can't do anything about Ram while Atanelle's suspicious," said Magramid, starting toward the House. "Just keep a watch on him for now."

"I wasn't talking about Ram," muttered Ty.

Suddenly a head-splitting boom crashed down upon the court. Magramid covered her ears in surprise, grimacing, until she realized her rain had been stopped.

"Go away!" she shrieked, turning on Jentessa.

"You murderer," cursed the other, advancing across the court. "You killed my Intermediator." Her graceful face was tight with rage and indignation. "You had no right. He was an innocent! You're—"

The rain returned with a vengeance, drowning Jentessa's words with the noise, until she raised her hand and dried the sky again. A burst of flame flew from her fingers to Magramid's hair, which flared for an instant before sizzling out.

"You're insane!" cried Jentessa, her caution lost in the fury.

"You've tortured this colony as you've tortured your own. I won't take it anymore. I won't have you killing my people, seducing my Ruler . . . *trying* to seduce my Ruler!" She let out a laugh. "Look at you! Your body's in ruins, yet still you presume to court his love."

Magramid's eyes, fixed hard all this while on her enemy, dropped at once to her wrinkled hands, staring at them in horror, as if seeing their deterioration for the first time.

"I will get my final vengeance," swore Jentessa. There was a frightening conviction to her voice that hadn't been there before, but Magramid didn't notice. "You're not the only one willing to take desperate measures. Just you wait and see." With a cry of fury, Jentessa spun about on the wet grass, sending water shooting up from the ground. Then she was gone.

After a moment, Ty uncovered his head to glance up at his mother, afraid of the anger he expected there; but Magramid wasn't angry. She was smiling, practically beaming, and the clouds above her began to separate.

"I've been a fool," she whispered. "A fool! Why didn't I realize? Cam can't see *me*, he hasn't seen *me* beneath this sagging skin!" She turned to Ty, her face lit with the answer. "He needs my youth to desire me. My beauty!"

Magramid crowed with delight, and spread out her arms to Cam's bedroom above the court. "Wait for me," she called to him. "I will be back!"

"Mother!" cried the wild man, but Magramid had faded down to the Center, deserting him again.

19

Kerk and Paragrin stood on the empty beach, watching the last of the fishing boats set out on the late-morning tide. The wind was strong, whipping their hair about and stinging their faces, but neither one of them thought to go back to the city; Paragrin needed the soothing horizon. For the same unexplainable reason, she had needed Kerk to come and share the comfort with her this morning.

"Isn't this glorious?" he exclaimed, throwing out his arms. "I could stay here forever! But if we do stay much longer, Paragrin," he said, turning serious, "I'll have to take a job. It's only right. Do you think they'd let me try sailing a boat?"

When she didn't answer, Kerk poked her with his thumb. "Do you think they'd let me?" he persisted. "Think how fine it will be if I can tell everyone back home that I sailed a boat!"

"I thought you didn't want to go home," said Paragrin quietly. "I thought you were going to stay here forever."

Kerk made a face. "What's the matter with you this morning?" he asked; then he grinned. "I know. You're afraid I like this place better than the Melde, aren't you?"

"Don't be ridiculous," said Paragrin. "Do you think I care

about your opinion? You, who can't look past your own navel!"

Kerk's jaw dropped.

"Oh, don't get ruffled," she said, reaching for his hand. "I didn't mean—"

"I know what you meant, and I've had enough of your judgment," he growled, throwing her off. "You invited me to come here, remember? *I* thought it was odd, you wanting to be such pals again, but I came, and I won't listen now to your insults." He turned to go back.

"Stay, please," she said, in a voice so soft that Kerk's anger was checked.

"What's wrong?" he asked again, peering at her—and then all at once he brightened. "I know! It's that time of month for you, isn't it? Ellagette used to act just this way."

Paragrin stared at him, incredulous.

"Of course," said Kerk, faltering, "it could be something more serious . . ."

"Will you let go of me!" said Atanelle, attempting to shake Ram off her arm. "I feel as if I've grown another limb."

Ram held firm, and glanced behind him apprehensively as they reached the top of the stairs in the Great House.

"If you won't let go, at least tell me why Ty's been following you," said Atanelle. "What were the three of you talking about last night in the storm?"

"Nothing," said Ram. "Just chatting."

"*Chatting?* Well, if that's all you have to say, you can just— Ow!" she cried. Ram had pinched her on the arm, for suddenly Ty was at the bottom of the stairs, watching them.

She sighed. "All right, relax. We'll go into the Ruler's room. At least he won't follow you there." With a swing of the deer-pelt curtain, Ty was lost to their view.

Aridda was there already when they entered. Cam looked up from his perch on the corner of the bed. He said nothing, but flinched in a queer way that made Atanelle wonder if all this company was depressing him, as if somehow he kept hoping it were Paragrin and Kerk, instead.

Aridda sensed it, too. "Just one more word and I'll let you be," she said. "I thought you'd like to know: the old woman didn't sleep in her room last night."

"She didn't?" Cam looked up at her, bewildered. "Where did she sleep?"

"I meant, she's gone completely," said Aridda. "I haven't seen her since the storm yesterday."

Cam's brow tightened. "How can she be gone? She wouldn't leave here without telling me."

The deer pelt moved aside again, but as Cam turned hopefully for Magramid, it was only her son who entered.

"You shouldn't be in here," said Cam, frowning.

Ram squeaked and hid behind the warrior.

"Should I remove him?" said Atanelle, leveling a hard stare at Ty, but Cam didn't answer her. He stood up from the bed and confronted him.

"Have you seen your mother?" he asked.

The wild man swung his gaze from Ram to the Ruler and narrowed it there, but he said nothing.

"Have you or have you not?" Cam said impatiently. "I'm in no mood for these games."

"Our friend has been acting very strangely," said Atanelle.

"More strangely than usual, that is. Ty's been following your grandfather all morning."

"No, he hasn't!" said Ram quickly, flashing an unconvincing smile to the room. "We've just been playing a little game, that's all."

"A game?" said Atanelle, turning on him. "For that I've been forced to keep you company!" She tried to shake him off again, but he clung to her tighter than ever.

Cam went up to the wild man, meeting him chest to chest. "Tell me where she is," he commanded, but still Ty said nothing, smiling at his rival with a smug defiance.

"We'll find her without you, then," said Cam, and turned away, his anger flushed on his face. "Atanelle, seek her out and take this . . . this *man* with you when you go. And send Notts here to talk to me. I'd go myself," he muttered, "but I don't think I can take walking through the crowds today."

"Notts isn't home," said Atanelle.

Ram's eyes popped as the wild man shot him a look, and he hid his face in the warrior's back.

"Notts is always there this time of the morning," said Cam.

"So I thought," said Atanelle, "but I went there myself not half an hour ago and he wasn't there. The Amulet is gone, too; that little holy box of his was left open and empty, and his floor is still wet from yesterday's storm, not cleaned up at all. It's strange, as if he just disappeared."

"Now this is ridiculous!" Cam declared. "Notts and Magramid can't both be missing. What are you people trying to do? Make my life more difficult than it already is? Don't bring me these reports of disappearances. *Find* them." He sat down on the bed, scowling. "Is it asking too much for you to take on a little responsibility just while I'm trying—in vain, it seems—to collect myself?"

"Of course not, my Ruler," said Atanelle. "I'll find them both. Alone." She tried to pry Ram's fingers from her arm. "I don't need you to find the others!" she barked.

"Don't leave me alone!" Ram pleaded in her ear. "The wild man will—" But he stopped short, staring at the door. Atanelle followed his gaze.

"When did Ty leave?" she asked, turning back to Cam.

"He's out waiting to jump me somewhere," Ram wailed. "Please, woman! If there's any mercy in that thick skull of yours—"

"Stop where you are," said Atanelle, and shook her head at his trembling. "You are a pitiful sight. Come on then, old man. I just hope you remember my great kindness when Ty's found some other 'game' to play."

"Yes, of course I will!" said Ram, following her to the door.

"Right . . ." said Atanelle, and they exited together.

Aridda turned to go as well, when she spotted the breakfast tray untouched on the bedside table. "You're not eating, Cam," she said. "It's no wonder you're pale as batter."

"Don't worry about me, Aridda," he muttered, rubbing his face wearily with his hand. "I don't need anyone to mother me."

Her jaw stiffened. "Well, you sure need someone," she said, and left the room.

Cam sat there on the corner of the bed in silence; then he lay back, slowly curling up on the blanket. A faint, familiar scent wafted up from the weave, a Paragrin scent, and a thousand memories of her came crowding to his mind. At first it was comforting; then they grew too strong for him and he tore the blanket from the bed, rising to his knees upon the matting. "Oh, Jentessa!" he whispered, stretching down his arms imploringly toward the Center. "I'm in pain. *Help me.* Break your vow of separateness again—just this once—and come to console me, to explain why it happened. Please! I've never felt so alone . . ." He squeezed his eyes shut, his fists clenched in desperation, but no gentle voice rose to soothe his fears, no graceful figure shimmered to a reassuring fullness before him. His mind only echoed with his own despair, and he fell to bury his face in the pillow, trying to drive the memories from his brain, alone.

"Well, if it's not the time of month, then what *is* wrong with you?" asked Kerk, following Paragrin toward the platforms where they had first discovered the people.

"It hasn't struck you at all, has it?" she accused, climbing onto one of them. "The strangeness of this place! The awful sense of foreboding that hovers in the air."

"The only thing that hovers is fish smell," said Kerk, jumping up after her. "What foreboding?"

"Magramid," said Paragrin. "Magramid! Don't you realize what she can do? What she's already done? Just because she's not here now, you're ignoring her. But these people don't forget. They live in her shadow constantly. And don't you think," said Paragrin, putting an arm on his shoulder, "that if she returns while we're here, she'll have a very special interest in *us*?"

"I'm surprised at you," said Kerk with a grin. "You actually believe all those stories that are floating around. I don't know if Half-Divines ever walked about in the old times," he said, "but I sure haven't seen any lately. This Magramid must be a legend, that's all, told to children to keep them in line. Or maybe she's just a crazy old woman who terrorizes this place. *I* don't know, but she's nothing for us to get worked up about. What?" he demanded, suddenly frowning at Paragrin. "Why are you looking at me like that?"

"Oh, Kerk . . ." she said, then caught herself. How could he know? She turned her back on the ocean and gazed at the wide-open mouth of the river behind them. "The stories about Magramid are true," she said firmly. "Half-Divines do exist, even today. I know they do." The wind from off the water blew her hair about her head. "Jentessa. Do you remember her?"

"The last Intermediator," said Kerk. "So?"

"She's one," said Paragrin, and glanced at him. "A Half-Divine. *Our* Half-Divine."

Kerk stared at her, then broke into another grin. "Right," he said.

"She proved it to me, and she proved it to your brother," said Paragrin. "Believe it or not. And now no one else knows her real identity, except you—and apparently every single person in *this* colony."

Kerk squinted as the sun's reflection off the grassy pools blazed out at him. "If what you say is true," he began, after a moment of uncomfortable consideration, "—and I'm not saying I believe it completely—then why would the Vasser know more about it than the Melde? That doesn't make any sense."

"I know," said Paragrin, "and that's what's worrying me. Nothing I held sacred makes any sense here. Jentessa is good! Caring; like a mother almost, to the Melde. But Magramid, she's . . . something altogether different. The Vasser people are so contemptuous of religion, and why not, considering? It's just shaken me, that's all, shaken my— what I understood to be the truth. I don't know." She shrugged. "I just want to get away from this place. I want to go home, where everything's more rational. Don't you want to go home, Kerk?" She turned to commiserate, but found him gone from her side, ambling down the platform toward the river mouth. "Kerk!" she shouted. "Were you even listening to me?"

"There's something caught out on a sandbar," he said. "I want to see what it is." He stepped off the platform and onto the edge of the river, his boots sinking in the muck.

Paragrin peered out to where he was heading. "Is it some sort of dead animal?" she said, taken with curiosity despite herself. She walked down the platform after him, trying to decipher the animal's shape.

Kerk waded out into the shallow depths. Paragrin saw how the thing was stuck on the sandbar, half its bulk lost among the tall grasses, while the other half still bobbed slightly in the current. She dropped into the river and came up behind Kerk.

Suddenly he pulled back, stumbling in the water. "Oh, my Maker!" he said. "It's a body."

Paragrin moved him aside to look. He was right. There were two human legs sticking out into the water. Paragrin raised her lip.

"Should we pull it out," she said, "or tell the others?"

"Let's see who it is," said Kerk, and took hold of the feet. "Maybe it's old Magramid come home at last!"

"That's not even funny," said Paragrin, and helped him haul it from the sandbar.

The face of the corpse dragged along the sand and then disappeared into the river. It rocked there, almost as if *it* were willing the movement instead of the current. Paragrin shuddered.

"The head hangs strangely," said Kerk. He began to reach toward the neck, but paused over a lump in the tunic instead. There was something caught in the torn and tangled cloth at its back. When he saw a bit of chain hanging out from it, Kerk gave a yank and pulled it free.

The body revolved with the force, finally revealing the white and bloodless face to the sun.

Paragrin stared down, horrified.

Kerk unwound the treasure he had plucked. "Look," he yelled. "Another Amulet!"

"Look here," said Paragrin, her voice gone thick in her chest. "It's Notts. Sweet Maker, what's happened in my colony?"

20

"It's Magramid," said Giles. "It has to be."

"How else would the drowned man have gotten my Oval?" exclaimed Hanna, lifting the Amulet from her chest to admire again. "It's a miracle it found a way back to me. Meridor, look!" She held the iron out to her daughter, who felt it eagerly. "It almost gives me faith," Hanna whispered.

"Rot you!" cried Paragrin, pushing up from her chair. "You have no right to be happy when you know Magramid's in my colony." Her breath came quickly. "She's *your* problem. Why did she go to the Melde?"

"I haven't a guess," replied Hanna coolly, "but I've been robbed of my Amulet for almost fifteen years. I think I deserve a little happiness."

"Not when one of my people has been murdered."

"*One* of your people?" said Hanna, the color rushing to her face. "What about the hundreds that have died here beneath her rule? It's about time the Melde learned a little of suffering. I would have sent Magramid there myself if I could have!"

Paragrin's lip trembled, but she didn't reply; instead, she took up her bow and quiver from beside the hearth.

"Come on, Kerk," she said quietly. "We haven't a second to lose."

Kerk looked uncertain as he slid his old blade into its sheath.

Hanna was silent, gazing down at the floor. Meridor looked from her to her uncle, who came forward, his gnarled fingers pulling at his beard.

"And just how do you think you'll stop a Half-Divine?" he asked Paragrin.

She adjusted her quiver against her back. "I don't know," she said, "but I'll kill her if I have to."

Giles laughed. Paragrin stared at him indignantly, then turned and found Kerk picking up his pack too slowly.

"What's the matter with you?" she shouted. "Are you coming with me or not?"

"Rot you, Paragrin, I was just thinking! You never give me the slightest credit for—"

And then Meridor gave a scream of frustration. It was so unexpected that everyone jumped and turned on her, demanding explanation. Meridor frowned disapprovingly, flipping her hair behind her.

"Well, *really*," she said. "I can't believe all the nastiness you four are tossing about. You're acting like children, and this isn't any time for games."

At first no one spoke, too surprised by the scolding; then Giles drew himself up and took Meridor roughly by the hand.

"You listen here, girl," he began.

"No, she's right," said Hanna, getting up from the table. "And I'm sorry for what I said, Paragrin. I wouldn't wish Magramid on anyone, let alone a friend."

"I wish I could be more happy for your Oval's recovery," muttered Paragrin.

"I understand," said Hanna. "I'd feel the same way you do if our places were reversed. Now, enough apology. We have to help you get home."

"There's nothing you can do," said Paragrin, "except wish us luck."

"Nonsense," said Hanna. "We can take you there." She turned and raised an eyebrow at her brother.

"How?" asked Paragrin.

"How?" asked Giles uneasily.

"By foot, it will take them forever," said Hanna. "By boat . . ."

"Boat?" said Giles.

"Boat!" Kerk brightened.

"That's absurd," exclaimed Giles. "Sail a boat upriver? That's impossible."

"Not for an expert sailor," said Hanna, "who knows how to manipulate wind . . . like you."

"They'd be caught upon the rocks in minutes," said Giles. "In the end, it would take longer! They'd end up on foot, anyway, if they both didn't perish first in the water. Now, that would be a fine start for a rescue, wouldn't it? Besides," he said, turning to Paragrin, "there's nothing you can do to stop Magramid. By foot or by boat, the end will stay the same."

"I can't just do nothing!" said Paragrin. "My mate is alone."

"You should have thought of that before you left him," said Giles. "If you'd known your duty—"

"Look who's talking 'duty,'" Hanna snapped, taking her brother by the arm. "You, who won't even help your fellow colony. Wasn't it you who said once how fine it would be if all the colonies united against the immortals? What finer chance do you have than now to prove your support?"

Giles said nothing, glaring down at her.

Hanna threw out her chin. "Then I'll take them myself," she declared.

"You! You wouldn't get them past the tall grass," said Giles.

"Well, at least I'll have tried to do my duty."

"All *right*," said Giles, slamming his fist upon the table. "I'll take them. But it's all for naught, I'm telling you!"

Kerk gave a whoop. "This is wonderful! I can't believe I'll be riding in a—" He stopped, his face suddenly stripped of its joy. "I have to say goodbye to Boon," he said.

"Then go do it now," said Paragrin, "and we'll meet you at the platforms." Kerk was off, and she turned to the others. "Thank you," she said, "for everything!"

"Don't thank us yet," returned Giles gruffly. "We may all end up in the wet as it is."

During the next hour, the company descended to the platform and, with much pushing and pulling, managed to get Giles's little boat past the sandbars and afloat in the mouth of the river, its polished mast standing tall, with the sail still folded, waiting. Everyone was waiting; Kerk had not reappeared.

Paragrin had climbed over the railing to sit on the bench that ran around the inside of the boat, leaving Meridor and Hanna waist-deep in the water and Giles impatient at the rudderwheel. Paragrin lifted her head to smell the new air—

that damp, earthy scent that told more of plantings than of fish. Her heartbeat quickened.

"We can't wait any longer," she said to Giles. "Kerk knew we had to leave. It'll serve him right to be left behind."

But then all at once a shout rang out from the shore. Kerk was there on the riverbank—with Boon at his side. Everyone watched them, surprised, as the two dove into the water together and resurfaced at the boat. Kerk hoisted the boy up to Giles, then scrambled up himself to sit beside him on the bench. Boon grinned, and Kerk draped a dripping arm around his little shoulders.

"What are all of you staring at?" said Kerk, glancing about at their faces. "Let's go. We're late starting as it is!"

"This isn't the time for jokes," said Paragrin crossly. "Put him off now or he goes with us all the way to the Melde."

"Of course he does," Kerk returned. There was a note of challenge in his newfound voice. "I'm all the boy has. I couldn't abandon him, could I?"

"That would have been irresponsible," said Boon. "I pointed it out to him myself."

Paragrin's eyebrow lifted.

"That's right," said Kerk. "Now stop your fidgeting, Boon; you'll need both your hands to hold on to the bench. Whenever you're ready," said Kerk, looking up again at their faces.

Paragrin shook her head in disbelief, and Giles lifted his weathered face to the sky. "The sail is out!" he cried, and swung the bottom pole down and around the mast, unfolding the cloth to the air.

"Have strong winds!" said Hanna, reaching up to Paragrin, "and give my best to Cam."

The two Rulers touched each other's hands for a moment, an Oval Amulet glinting on each of their chests. Then the cloth caught the wind, and with a jolt, the little vessel took off.

"Come back safe!" Hanna called to her brother as he bid her farewell.

"Meridor's waving," said Paragrin.

"So?" Kerk grinned at her. "Isn't this a thrill?" he said to Boon. The boy laughed as a spray of water leapt up into the boat.

Paragrin watched them for a moment, then turned, clinging to the railing. She felt envious suddenly of their closeness, and wondered, as the ocean fell farther and farther behind her, if there would be anyone left at home for *her* to hold.

21

"Now, isn't this a cheery sight?" said Atanelle brightly as she accompanied Cam through the bustling streets. She and Aridda had conferred, and decided that after his two days of self-enforced seclusion they had to push Cam into the sunshine and out of himself.

This was the first attempt.

"Take him to see Ellagette," Aridda had suggested. "He might feel less inhibited with her, seeing as she already knows, and such. And it could help him feel stronger, being able to offer a shoulder for her to cry on if she needed it."

Atanelle didn't think that Ellagette would need it; for all her daintiness, Ellagette had a very tough skin and felt things, the warrior suspected, rather less than Cam. Still, it had seemed a good plan—they were at a loss for what else to do for him.

"Isn't this cheerful?" Atanelle offered again, but Cam didn't hear her, too intent as he was on the threat of the crowds. He had fixed a kind of smile on his face when they had left, an all-purpose reaction that he hoped would do in place of any talking. Atanelle frowned, and noted with some worry that this unnatural expression was drawing more whispers than acceptance. She decided in that moment to make this excursion as brief as possible. She led him on, faster, toward the weaver's.

"How am I to keep up with you if you're running like a maddened rabbit?" complained a voice from behind.

"I didn't ask you along," returned Atanelle, casting an irritable look at Ram. "You don't need my protection anymore, old man. Ty hasn't followed you all day."

"And you think that means something," said Ram. "Well, you just wait until I'm murdered. Then you'll be sorry!"

Atanelle had to bite her tongue to keep from correcting him, but she was determined to make things as peaceful as possible. She put out a hand, gently, to guide Cam onto the street where the craftspeople had their shops. He seemed to have forgotten where he was going, moving like a sleepwalker through his own city. And yet there was nothing else about him that suggested sleep; his movements were stiff and restrained, he was so careful not to bump against another person, as if in fear that all the churning inside him would explode.

"We're here," said Atanelle, stopping him in front of the weaver's shop. "I'll just slip in and ask Ellagette to come and—"

"I want to wait inside," said Cam.

These were the first words he had spoken since they left the House, and Atanelle didn't argue. She led him to the little foyer just within the entrance, then went deeper into the shop to find Ellagette among the looms.

Ram hovered in the foyer, too, and peered up at Cam. "I don't see why you're so miserable," he said. "I lost more than you: in just the past year, a son, a grandson, and now a granddaughter, too. You don't see me feeling sorry for myself."

A dull look of disgust, uncommon to Cam's face, found residence there now. Ram was offended, and when the warrior returned with Ellagette, he willingly quit the young man's company to wait outside with Atanelle.

"So. How are you?" asked Cam after an uncomfortable silence.

"All right," said Ellagette. "Surprised to find you here. You look awful, Cam. Have you been sleeping at all?"

"Not much," he said.

"I haven't either," Ellagette sighed. "I suppose I don't look any better."

"Not much," said Cam, and after a moment they laughed. "I've been worried about you," he said. "I meant to visit sooner . . ."

"Oh, I've been fine. Work has helped to keep my mind off things." She nodded toward the rows of looms behind her in the shop. "I've never been so productive. The weave-master is beginning to notice."

They laughed again; then Ellagette crossed her arms. "How much longer are you going to keep silent, Cam?" she asked. "You're going to tell the people soon, aren't you?"

"Do you wish that I would?"

"Well, actually, no," she said, and unfolded her arms, twisting a lock of her long dark hair around her fingers. "But it's just for a selfish reason. Kerk's presence has always been good protection for me. Even in his absence, his strength—and his relation to you—has usually helped to keep the other men away."

Cam took her hand. "Is someone bothering you?" he said. "Report him to me at once! Ellagette, you're like a sister to me. I—"

"I know," she said, interrupting him. "I didn't mean to worry you. It's not worth you scolding anyone for. Kerk's approach was always more—"

"More what?" demanded Cam. "More violent?"

"Your way is more civilized," said Ellagette gently, "but not as immediate. Now, don't worry. I'll be fine. I'm sorry I said anything. I should go back to my work before the master notices I'm gone." Cam nodded, squeezing her hand once more before she pulled away.

"Did everything go all right?" Atanelle asked, putting a hopeful face into the foyer. "Are you ready to go home?"

"I suppose," said Cam, but he felt somehow hesitant, as if he had unfinished business. He glanced back to where Ellagette had taken her place at the looms, and watched as the master, reemerging from the back, ambled over to speak to her. Cam couldn't hear what he said, but there was something disturbing about it: Ellagette leaned too attentively over the threads, as though she was trying to get away from him. And then the master leaned closer and slid his arm around her waist, his hand reaching toward her bosom.

In an instant the blood rushed to Cam's face. He bound into the shop's interior and seized the master, turning him around and felling him with one indignant blow.

"Cam!" gasped Ellagette. "What have you done?"

Atanelle ran into the shop, looking astoundedly from Cam to the victim, in utter disbelief at the scene.

Cam himself was incredulous. He stared down at the weavemaster, his arms outstretched, imploring. "I'm sorry," he said. "I—I don't know what—"

And then, unable to bear the eyes upon him, he broke from the shop without another word and ran home to his sanctuary.

When the business at the weaver's was resolved, Atanelle went back to the Great House to speak to Cam. She deposited Ram—still following her—at the bottom of the stairs, and went up alone to find her Ruler back on the corner of the bed, his fingers tangled in his hair.

"What's happening to me?" he murmured. "I'm going mad."

"Don't be ridiculous," said Atanelle.

Cam looked up at her, his torn knuckle held in front of him as evidence. "Today I struck someone for no reason," he said.

"According to Ellagette, you had reason."

"Even if I did, I don't go about using violence as a punishment. I don't *believe* in violence." He said this quietly, as if remembering an old conviction.

"Don't be so hard on yourself," said Atanelle. "You can't come out of a week like this unchanged. No one but you would expect it. Your mate and your brother have died," she said gently. "Forgive yourself a little insanity."

"That's easy for you to say," muttered Cam, rising to walk about the chamber. "You're not responsible for the colony's state of mind."

"I'm only saying what you would," she returned. "Remember: nothing is unforgivable."

Cam sank wearily again on the bed corner. "I'm not even sure I believe that anymore. I feel so lost, and it's not only Paragrin and Kerk; it's Notts, too, and Magramid. Where could they have gone to? It's been two days. I should be making decisions! When do I break the news to the people? And where do I find another Ruler? Sweet Maker, I don't even have a Holy Intermediator anymore to help me."

"I'll help you," said Atanelle quietly.

"I'm so afraid that Magramid and Notts are dead, too," Cam whispered. "And I can't lose anyone else! I'm losing myself as it is."

"No, you're not," said Atanelle firmly. "I won't let you. I don't know how to govern the colony, my Ruler, and I wouldn't try; I'm just a warrior. But whenever you need some strength to draw on, look for it here. Paragrin's last order to me was to look out for you," she said, "and I'll stand by while you're getting on your feet again, every difficult moment. I know you'll feel stronger soon! If there's any comfort to be had," said Atanelle, "it's that we've come through the worst of it."

A faint smile broke across Cam's face, and he gave her hand a squeeze. "You know," he said, "I almost believe you."

And then a scream rang out from below.

Magramid had returned.

22

Ram had been the first to see her. She faded up right in front of him in the entrance hall, and shocked the breath so completely out of his body that he couldn't utter a sound for several seconds; then he screamed. And when she turned her youthful face toward him and looked through those too-familiar, too-bright eyes, he screamed again at whom he thought he saw transformed before him. It was all of it too fantastic, and he fainted in a bony heap beneath the tapestries.

Magramid cast him a scornful look, and after a second of impatient meditation, she sensed her lover's presence above and turned her steps toward the stairway, her smooth hand gliding delicately along the stony wall.

Atanelle rushed out of the chamber, expecting to find the old leader clutched in the hands of the wild man. What she saw instead was a young girl with fine brown hair and skin so pale and unweathered it looked new. She cocked her head in confusion, which grew more intense as the girl's expression fixed upon her and hardened.

"What are you doing?" asked Atanelle as the girl was climbing the last of the stairs. "You can't come up here."

The girl stood, defiant, on the landing. Atanelle frowned

and reached to push her back, when the girl shot out her hand and seized the other's wrist with such force that the warrior cried out in pain.

"Atanelle," said the girl, "my stalwart friend, let me pass and go to him—now!—or I'll crush you right here on the stones." Atanelle gaped up at her, stunned, as the girl's inhuman strength forced her slowly to her knees.

"Great Maker," Cam gasped, as he stopped, paralyzed, at the bedchamber door.

"Cam!" the girl exclaimed, her new complexion blushing with anticipation. "I've come back to you at last." She threw off Atanelle with such a violent snap of her arm that the warrior's head struck the wall, and she was silenced.

The girl advanced. "You know me now, don't you, my loveling?" she said, forcing Cam back to the chamber. "How I've waited for this moment. Now at last you can desire me as I've desired you, each of us beautiful in our youthful skin."

Cam stared at the eyes, the shape of the mouth, his heartbeat intensifying with every familiar feature. "Magramid," he said. "I can't believe it . . ." Dread washed over him to see this motherly figure so utterly changed.

"Come now, don't look so frightened," she said gently, reaching to caress his shoulder. "You, at least, should be unimpressed by our Half-Divine ways; you, who knew my sister so well."

"Jentessa!" Cam's heart soared with sudden hope. "Where is she? Jentessa!"

Magramid shook her head. "She doesn't believe in interfering; you know that. She told me herself that her playing at Holy Intermediator was an exception. But what matter? We have no need of her here. Cam, we are better than she is. You are better, more accepting than the Maker Itself! Why do you think I chose you for my lover?" Her eyes shone. "I knew such uncondemning kindness only once before. Can you guess with whom?" She gazed into his stricken face. "With Ty's father . . . and for the second time in all my interminable life, I am about to reward this kindness with the gift of my immortal passion."

"No!" Cam thrust out his hand to stop her. "Magramid, you misunderstood!"

"I misunderstood?"

"That kindness," said Cam, easing his voice and hand from resistance, "I would have shown to anyone. It meant nothing."

"Nothing?" Magramid flushed. "No one gives for nothing! Don't say I misread your attentions, Cam, or that you ever misunderstood mine. I took care of both obstacles to our love: first, Paragrin, and now my age."

Cam's eyes widened.

"I understand why you were reluctant to seduce me," said Magramid, smiling, reaching out again toward him. "Inside I burned, but all you saw was my shell, my old withered skin. How could you have wanted me as freely as I wanted you? But I renewed myself! I became young and beautiful once more—for you."

"What did you do to Paragrin?" Cam cried, breaking from his stance. "Did you kill her? Was it you who killed her?"

Magramid stepped back, surprised.

"If you killed her, I swear," Cam bellowed, "I'll kill *you!*"

He rushed toward Magramid, seizing her by the throat.

But Magramid pried his fingers off, throwing him down. "I did what I had to," she shouted, "for our love!"

"You don't know what love is," he countered, scrambling to his feet again. "You don't love me, and you never loved that other man. All you feel is some selfish, malignant lust. I could never love you, Magramid."

Magramid's mouth fell. She looked, disbelieving, at the man whose hot defiance melted now into sorrow, his shoulders bent and shaking.

"What have you done?" Cam sobbed. "What have you done to Paragrin? To my life? *Damn* you, Magramid. Damn you!"

Magramid stared at him. "My Maker . . ." she breathed. "You're no different from the others, after all, are you? You're as hateful as the rest of them, as hateful as Jentessa. It's no wonder she chose you for a ruler," she said, her voice rising. "You're just like her!"

"Oh, please, Jentessa!" Cam threw down his arms to the Center. "Jentessa, come to me . . ."

"Damn yourself," growled Magramid, trembling with rage. "You idiot, you mortal! Do you think it matters in the end what you feel? What you want or don't want? I can take what I choose. My gifts can be given as punishment as well as reward." A terrible darkness stole across her face, and she took a step toward him.

Cam stumbled backward, putting the bed between them, calling out again to his old friend, his protector. How could Jentessa not come? How could she not care?

Magramid still came, forcing him beyond the bed to the wall.

"No . . ." Cam whispered as the truth of his abandonment struck him low at last. There would be no rescue; he was left—naked in his humanness—to the mercy of this greater, awful power. Never had he felt so afraid.

When she touched him, he tried to push her back, striking out at her wildly, struggling in her hold. But Magramid was deaf to his wishes now. She overpowered him easily, and silenced his final cries with a kiss.

At the muddy bank of the river, the little boat from the Vasser ground to a breathless stop; in fact, the wind drew itself from the sail just as the boat reached the bank, as if it knew as well as the passengers where they were supposed to get off.

"This has been the most extraordinary trip," Giles gushed as he folded the sail quickly around the mast. "I've never known such remarkable luck with wind! We couldn't have been more fortunate if the Maker had sent us here Itself."

"That may be close to the truth," said Paragrin, taking up her bow and quiver to leap to the shore. Jentessa was behind their unnatural progress, she was sure of it, proving once again the obvious: that the Melde's Half-Divine was dependably good and true. It wasn't too late to save her city; she had faith in that. She had faith.

"Wait for us!" Kerk shouted as he lifted Boon to the bank, but Paragrin had already sped through the entrance into the court.

"What a weird tall place this is," said Boon, and he wrinkled his nose; "and everything smells like mud."

"Don't worry—you'll learn to like it," said Kerk, helping Giles to fasten the boat to a root growing from the bank.

"But for now we have business to do. This way!" he called, and led the two strangers into his city.

Paragrin stood, transfixed, in the middle of the court. Everywhere around her life progressed just as normally as it had when she left. Crouched in a fighting position, her bow clutched in her fist, she began to feel terribly ridiculous. No one was even noticing her; no one fell to their knees before her in gratitude for her timely arrival. She straightened, a look of intense annoyance coming over her, and started to walk more leisurely toward the House, when all at once a figure bolted from the entrance and knocked her down.

"Holy thunder!" gasped Ram when he recognized his victim. "You're alive! I knew it. I knew it!" He fell upon her there on the grass and began kissing her hand.

"What are you doing?" Paragrin swore, yanking her arm away from his affections. "Since when did you crawl into the light again?" She stood up, bow in hand, and glared at her grandfather. "Have you been causing trouble? Because if you have—"

"Me? Me?" said Ram. "This is no time for prejudice, rot you! She's back, and we'll perish, all of us, if you don't stop her."

"She? She who?" Paragrin's body tensed again. She grabbed his arm, shaking him. "Is Magramid here? Where? Tell me!"

"In there!" he wailed, looking at the House. "At least she was when I saw her last. I was overpowered!"

Paragrin bolted for the entrance, leaving him babbling behind her.

"She tried to kill me!" shouted Ram, playing more now

178

to the people who were starting to stare at him than to Paragrin. "She's inhuman. A freak! Just appearing in front of me like a bolt of lightning. I fought her like a bear, but she had incredible strength, and—"

"There's Paragrin," said Giles, pointing toward the head of the court, where Paragrin was just disappearing into the House.

"Let's follow her then," said Kerk, starting forward, "though it's funny that no one seems particularly—" He stopped abruptly, caught in speechless admiration of a person who stood near them in the court. Boon looked up at him, wondering, then followed his gaze to a pretty young woman with long black hair and a shocked expression.

His mission forgotten, Kerk ran to embrace her. At first Ellagette started back in fright; then, as her disbelief melted into sweet acceptance, she threw her arms around him and wept for joy.

"Bother," said Boon, looking on with annoyance. "Here we go again."

Giles went on alone into the House. Paragrin was there, emerging from the dining room into the entrance hall, shouting Magramid's name. "I haven't found her yet!" she said.

Within the Rulers' chamber, where she held Cam fast between herself and the wall, the Half-Divine turned her head to listen. When she heard a footfall on the stairs, she spat in anger and swung Cam, unobtained, to the bed.

"I'll be back," she said.

At last alone, Cam lay crumpled on the blanket, unable to move. His shirt was ripped open, his flesh stung, his mouth burned where she had been kissing him—but this was not the worst of his injuries. He was sick, repulsed by his own skin, as if he couldn't ever hope to expunge from it the memory of her touch. He had almost passed out from the nausea when a familiar voice shouting from below roused him. His eyes flew open. His heart pounding, he struggled to push himself up from the bed.

Magramid stood at the top of the stairs, startled by Paragrin's sudden appearance. She froze, uncertain of what to do.

Paragrin was no less startled, although less surprised, to see *her*. There she was—the unholy daughter revealed at last! Never had there been such an ugly difference between innocent look and jaded essence; the ancient, more complicated soul betrayed in the burning eyes. Paragrin took a step backward from those eyes, her bow held with less assurance.

Magramid smiled at the retreat. She moved her stare for the moment to Giles, who was struck by this first sight of her metamorphosis. He put a hand out to Paragrin protectively when she stood back beside him.

The Half-Divine relaxed. "Welcome, Paragrin," she said in her girlish voice; but like the eyes, it betrayed a more dangerous tone. "I've just been enjoying a visit with your mate."

Paragrin flushed, and tore an arrow from her quiver. Released from her fear, she started up the steps, fitting the arrow to the string. "What have you done to him?" she demanded, aiming her weapon at Magramid. "Stand aside. Now! Or I'll kill you, I swear it."

Magramid laughed so cruelly then that Paragrin let the

arrow fly. The Half-Divine caught it and snapped it in two between her hands.

"My Maker," said Paragrin, awed, and backed down again. Giles's fringe of beard trembled.

"You are all so foolish!" Magramid cried in amazement. "You think you can hurt me, can control my actions. Jentessa's done you a big disservice by hiding our powers. Haven't you told her, Giles, how easily I hold the Vasser to my will?" A spark of fire erupted on the man's sleeve, and Paragrin gasped as he slapped it out.

"Cam was just as foolish," said Magramid. "Why don't you come up here, Paragrin," she said, "and see how easily I work my will with him."

Paragrin cried in fury and threw aside her bow, ready to rush up at the Half-Divine again, when all at once *he* stumbled out from the bedchamber and their eyes met.

"Cam!" she whispered.

He gazed down at her in disbelief. "It *was* your voice I heard!" he said. "Dear love . . ."

Magramid scowled at this joyous reunion. "Get back," she shouted to Cam. "I haven't finished with you yet," and she shoved him toward the chamber.

Paragrin would have flown at her herself for this outrage if the dazed but dauntless Atanelle hadn't risen at that moment from the landing and seized the unsuspecting villain. Together, they spun and rolled down the steps in a riotous tumble.

Paragrin leapt out of their path just in time, and seeing her mate unguarded at last, she met Cam halfway up the stairs, wrapping him so tightly in her arms that he could barely breathe; but what did he care for breath?

"You're alive! Oh, Paragrin, you're alive," he exclaimed, and held her even tighter.

Below them the battle continued. Both Giles and Atanelle were hard at work keeping Magramid from the Rulers. Alone, neither one of the mortals could have kept her from her purpose; together, they seemed to be succeeding. They struck such a balance—already the strategy was understood: Atanelle, taking care of the grosser assaults; Giles making use of distraction and sacrifice when she was momentarily disabled. But this luck couldn't last; Magramid finally felled them both and advanced, little impaired, toward the lovers.

Behind her, wrapped in a hooded cloak, an anxious figure hovered in the entryway, her eyes wide with anticipation of glory. She had waited for this moment for so long— one little death!—and the scourge of the Half-Divines and of the world would be exiled forever. One little death . . . but why did it have to be Paragrin's?

The Rulers clung together, backing up the steps as Magramid advanced.

"You can't escape me," she assured them, her breath coming quickly, "neither one of you."

Cam pushed Paragrin behind him. "Leave my mate alone," he said. "You don't want her."

"Cam!" cried Paragrin.

"Leave her and my colony alone and I'll go with you, Magramid. I'll give you anything you want."

"It's too late! I don't want your love anymore," said Magramid, "only your misery. I want you to suffer the way I have suffered." She forced them slowly to the landing. " 'Nothing is unforgivable,' right, my sweet Cam?" she said. "Then forgive *this*."

Magramid shot out her hands and, knocking Cam aside, took the hated rival in her murderous arms at last. Paragrin screamed, struggling in her hold, but the iron-like fingers found their way to her neck, compressing, compressing, until an anguished voice rang out from below.

"Stop!"

Magramid spun around and saw her as she threw back the concealing hood from her cloak.

Jentessa.

23

"Enough!" cried Jentessa, and hurled a dagger of fire toward her sister. Magramid shrieked, releasing her prey, and threw herself against the wall to smother her clothes.

Cam grabbed Paragrin back again, cradling her in his arms. "She's come!" said Paragrin. "I knew she'd come."

Below them in the entrance hall, Giles looked in admiration at the strong and graceful figure of Jentessa, but Atanelle's mouth fell open.

My Maker, she thought. It seems everyone's resurrected today! Then her eyebrows lifted as she began to suspect that her knowledge of Jentessa had been somewhat limited.

Another bolt of fire flew toward the enemy. "Leave my colony alone!" Jentessa shouted.

Magramid twisted away from the flame just in time, stumbling onto the stairs. "You still think you command me?" she howled. "You still think you're superior?" She struck back, sending two bolts flaring toward Jentessa. Giles ducked as one whizzled past him. "Damn you!" shrieked Magramid, and sent two more. Jentessa's cloak suddenly burst into flame, and the mortals in the hall cried out.

But Jentessa was not lost to them; in fact, to protect them

from the escalating warfare, she turned and fled from the House, trailing fire sparks behind her. Smoke billowed back into the hall, and Magramid flew down the stairs and followed. The mortals stared at one another, then ran after the sisters.

Jentessa led her pursuer into the court, her fiery cloak scattering the startled crowd. When the mortals came out of the House, the bright day had already changed: rain was pounding down from the sky with great crashes of thunder. People fled to the edges of the court, panicked, but the remnants of Jentessa's cloak dropped, extinguished, to the ground, and as quickly as they had come, the clouds disappeared. The sisters confronted each other, equal again, on the grass.

Then Magramid clenched her fists and the earth began to rumble. A wail went up from the people as once more the ground beneath their feet betrayed them. Pottery, just recently repaired, shattered anew, and the colonists fell prostrate on the ground, praying for salvation.

The unholy daughter alone stood firm. Jentessa had fallen, but now she struggled up and caused a force of wind to erupt into the court. Magramid stumbled; the earth tremors stopped. She cried out in fury and reached toward her sister through the deafening wind, her fine brown hair whipping about her head . . .

. . . And when they touched, when they clasped each other in a final venomous embrace, all the strength of their power was unleashed upon the colony. A clamorous rainstorm hammered from the sky, striking the cowering bodies like hailstones. Branches snapped; small trees were uprooted in the hurricane wind. Fire shot out from the sisters' clash, sparking into the air before the water beat it down again, and the earth trembled so violently that the foundation of the Great House itself threatened to break apart.

Even in the midst of her fury, Jentessa knew she was endangering the Melde. Her reason prevailed. She pulled away from the cataclysmic hold and, with heaving breath, stood apart, stretching her arms in supplication to the Center below.

"Essai!" she cried. "Maker of all on earth and within, you know your daughter Magramid is a demon! You have seen her try to desecrate my city, tyrannize her colony. Now at last you have caught her at her lowest and most foul level: she has tried to murder one of your blessed Rulers. The sacred law must be upheld, and she condemned!"

"I did not break the law!" exclaimed Magramid, starting toward Jentessa. "The Ruler is not dead." She pointed to Paragrin. "There my absolution lives!"

"You *meant* to kill her," said Jentessa. "If I hadn't stopped you—"

"If you hadn't stopped me . . ." Her eyes shone. "Thank the Maker, you kept me from my sin."

Jentessa flushed. "You will be condemned for the attempt, just as if you had succeeded! There is very little virtue dividing them."

"There is just virtue enough," said Magramid. "Let's see how the Maker decides it . . ."

The sisters faced each other across the court. In an awful silence, they waited for a verdict; while all around them, half buried in the refuse of their battle, the mortals lay, helpless pawns in this greater game.

The sisters waited. And waited. And then at last a triumphant smile broke across Magramid's face.

"Nothing," she said. "I won. Who is it who knows the Maker Essai so well? Not you, Jentessa. You still think It cares what we do. You're as deluded as this poor fool"— she nodded toward Cam—"who thought you cared enough to rescue him from my punishment . . . Both wrong! Both putting blind faith in an indifferent power.

"But enough," she exclaimed, smiling at her sister. "The storm has passed. The Melde is not perfection, Jentessa! Your Rulers are as petty as mine, only more self-righteous, like you. They're just like you. This colony wearies me, and I will quite happily return to my Vasser. Now we can go back to the way we were before: you in your settlement and me in mine."

"It cannot be the way it was before," Jentessa said, her eyes darkening. "I will not permit you to continue your tyranny."

"*You* won't permit?" said Magramid. "You sound so mutinous! I approve, for I always suspected that our morals were not so far apart, Jentessa. You think I glory in the Maker's mediocrity? I am as disgusted as you are, only less surprised."

From somewhere deep within the earth, a rumble broke upon the surface, making the ground tremble beneath the sisters' feet. Jentessa's eyes widened, but Magramid was unimpressed.

"See how a scolding makes my sister shake," she said. "What a coward you are, to talk rebellion one moment and quail the next! *I* do not fear the Maker. It has never cared what I do, and I do not care for It."

The earth shook again, harder, and Jentessa, struggling to keep her balance, called across to her sister, "Does this tell you It doesn't care?"

"It's bluffing," returned Magramid, "or It's even more dull than I had thought, to imagine this would frighten me."

The ground shook so violently then that Magramid was knocked to her knees.

"All right!" she shouted, losing her temper at last. "If you are so eager to communicate with me, my Maker, I'll meet you essence to essence. You can have your say in the Center before I go home to the Vasser." Magramid picked herself up again and, seeing a touch of satisfaction in her sister's face, went to reassure her.

"I am not at all concerned," said Magramid, "and will see you at some later unhappy time. Until then!"

Magramid threw out her arms toward the rumbling Center and closed her eyes. The mortals raised their submissive gazes in breathless suspense for another miracle as Magramid began her fade. Her thickness shrank to a shimmering—but just as she was nearly gone, the earth shook one last time. Her image returned in an unnatural rush to its heavy substance and was thrown, shrieking, to the grass.

The crowd gasped. Slowly, Magramid lifted her head, her eyes round with astonishment and fury.

"What—does—this—mean?" she demanded, her fingers splayed out upon the dirty ground. There was silence without in the mortal world, but within the earth the message was clear and final.

"You fool," said Magramid. "How dare you banish me . . . *Me!* Who is more honest in her soul than any of your other children. Who is more honest than you yourself, Essai. Damn your*self*, Essai!"

Jentessa fell back at the blasphemy, keeping her distance from her maddened sister as Magramid drew herself up to press her feet defiantly against the earth.

"Damn yourself, Essai," she said again. Her voice came as a whisper now, trembling with unloosened force like breeze before a storm. "I can do without you, without your Center—without another body! What do I need a body for? To remind me I am only half-divine? No! I will be *all* divine!" The passion in her broke at last; she threw back her head and sent sparks shooting through the court. "I will not stay in your realm anymore, Essai. I willingly consent to be exiled to a new, unexplored dimension. You keep the earth!" she cried. "I'll take the *sky!* And we'll see between us who wins more souls."

With a piercing scream, she spun herself about so fast that a great wind twisted up, lifting her bodily off the ground. Below her feet a ball of flame exploded; a thick coil of smoke shot high into the air, and from somewhere far above the court, an iron Rectangle—Giles's lost Amulet—fell back to the grass. As the smoke dissolved, Magramid was gone, leaving only a scorched bit of cloth hovering in the breeze.

The people stared fearfully into the sky, which crackled once with lightning before quieting again. Whether Jentessa still saw it as quiet she did not say.

And then the silence was ripped by a mournful wail. Staggering up from where he had been lying buried in the crowd, Ty reeled into the middle of the court and pushed

Jentessa aside, swearing at her through his sobs. He grabbed the bit of floating cloth, pressing it to his lips, and struggled desperately to spin into the sky after his mother.

But the half-man, weighed down with mortality, only fell with an anguished moan back to earth.

24

"*Jentessa!*" *cried Paragrin,* starting up as the wild man ran from the crowds. She hurried to embrace the Half-Divine, but Cam stood apart, watching his beleaguered people rise slowly to their feet. His colony once again lay ravaged by storm and vengeance. All repairs were torn apart, and new casualties littered the ground. He sank onto his haunches, picking up a broken branch whose blossoms had been torn from their stems by the wind. He turned it in his hand, the threads of his tattered shirt fluttering in the breeze.

"Cam?" Paragrin came back to him. "It's Jentessa." She looked at him, wondering at his silence, as he rose but did not speak.

The Half-Divine regarded her old friend with equal uncertainty. He would not meet her gaze, his eyes downcast, his mouth set against any words that might escape. When Jentessa reached out to him, Cam pulled from her touch, turning his head.

Paragrin stared at him.

Then: "This is a fine welcome you give us!" came a hearty voice, and Cam, his expression transformed instantly to joy, turned to find his brother standing there beside him.

"Kerk!" he cried.

"Who else?" Kerk said with a laugh, and he threw his arms around him. "I heard that you thought I was dead! You should have known no one ever gets the best of me."

"You're right. I should have known!" Cam gazed at his younger brother in amazement and smiled. "It doesn't matter now. It's over. I have you back." He took hold of Kerk's hand and turned to his mate. "Both of you back. I couldn't ask for more. Oh, Paragrin . . ."

He reached for her, and Kerk was just relinquishing his other hand when suddenly he seized Cam back again and spun him around. Cam lost his balance and landed on the grass with Kerk on top of him.

"What are you doing?" he said with a laugh. All at once a familiar wail cut through the murmur of the crowd. Every-one turned, and there was the wild man back by the House, clasping his head at the failure before him: for his enemy Cam sat up, still living—and in his arms was only the martyred body of the brother, a knife lodged in his side.

Ellagette screamed. For a second Kerk's eyes blinked open. He gripped Cam's shoulder; then his handsome face tensed and all expression fell from him. His grip relaxed.

Cam stared down in disbelief. The next moment the brothers were set upon, surrounded by people reaching for Kerk, calling to each other in high voices. Boon burst into tears, trying to touch his fallen hero as Giles and Atanelle lifted Kerk up, and Jentessa put her arms out to receive him.

"No!"

Suddenly Cam was on his feet, knocking the Half-Divine away. "Haven't you done enough?" His face was twisted, so filled with bitter rage that Jentessa stepped back from the body.

Cam stood bristling for another second, defending his insensate brother from her inhuman touch; then he spun around to see the half-man running from the court toward the forest. He let out a murderous yell and lurched after him.

"*Cam!*" cried Paragrin.

But Jentessa took her hand. "Let him go," she said firmly. "It's not Cam who needs help now; it's Kerk."

Paragrin turned and saw Kerk being taken into the House, his limbs hanging from the carriers' arms.

"Oh, Jentessa," she said, "he's going to die, isn't he?"

25

"*Now go, all of you,*" said Jentessa, when Kerk had been placed on the bed upstairs. "I'll need bandages, lots of them, with hot water and the herb cresserote." She lifted back the blood-soaked shirt while everyone scattered, and then pressed her palm firmly against the wound to stay the flow.

Ellagette was the last one to the door, and she turned when the others had gone, falling to her knees before Jentessa. "He'll live, won't he?" she said. "You can heal him?"

"He's lost a great deal of blood."

"But *you* can save him!" Ellagette's pale hands rose, trembling, to touch her. "Please," she said, "I couldn't bear to lose him again."

"Even a Half-Divine can't pull a man back from death," said Jentessa. She looked away, reaching with her free hand to move back the damp curls from Kerk's brow. He was cold, and when Ellagette touched him, she gasped.

"He's dead!"

"Quiet! Would you bury him already? Go find the others if you want to help him. Tell them to hurry."

Ellagette pushed herself up. As soon as she reached the door, Giles and Atanelle were there with bandages. A second behind them came Paragrin with the water. Aridda arrived moments later with a clutchsack of herb.

"This is all the cresserote in the House," said Aridda. Jentessa weighed the herb in her hand and smelled it to judge its potency. "I could try to find more in the outer colony," said Aridda, "if it's not enough."

"If this isn't enough," said Jentessa, "then there won't be cresserote in the land to save him." She glanced up. "You know something of medicine?"

Aridda bit her lip. "A little," she said, "but I don't know if I—"

"Stay in case I have need of you," said Jentessa. "The rest, leave us to our work."

"Can't I—" began Paragrin.

"No." Jentessa didn't even turn to speak to her. Paragrin peered at Kerk's immobile face and tried to see his grin upon it; that only made her feel worse.

Boon was at the door as she went to leave, and Paragrin took his hand to move him, but the boy wrenched free and ran to his silent friend, burying his head by the wound.

"Get the child away!" barked Jentessa, and Ellagette scooped him in her arms, pulling him back. He yelled out and called Kerk's name, and she pressed his head to her bosom.

"I won't leave Kerk," she said, rubbing her cheek on Boon's hair. He looked up at her, pleading. "Neither one of us will," she said quietly.

Jentessa turned to glare at her, yet met such an unyielding pair of eyes that she held in her words. She dipped the porous clutchsack in the water, making a paste of its contents.

"All right," said Jentessa, "if you stay where you are, away from the bed. If you can't manage it, I'll have Atanelle drag you out."

Ellagette stroked Boon's curls. He slipped his arms around her waist and watched as the two women worked on his friend.

"Aridda, when I take my hand from his wound I want you to set the paste against it. Quickly," said Jentessa.

Aridda's lips were red from her biting them, but she took the sack and exposed its contents, ready.

The forest would have been a good place to hide in— for a clever man. But Ty ran so clumsily: broken twigs and branches proclaimed his passage everywhere he went. Cam barely had to use his tracking skills to follow him, that half-man, that murderer Ty. Cam was possessed with the hunt, freeing his head from everything but this; especially from the eyes that fluttered in his mind, fluttered and closed. He would kill the man. It would be easy.

The afternoon shadows made a patchwork of the forest light. In and out of the sunshine Cam pursued him, getting closer and closer to his prey, until the wild man knew there was no escape. With nothing left to lose, Ty turned and confronted his foe.

Cam did not even pause in his mission. He flew at the wild man and knocked him to the ground, beating him again and again with his fists. The skin on Ty's face tore apart, and still Cam struck out at him, until the wild man thrust his fingers at Cam's eyes and he let him go.

Ty struggled up and tried to pin Cam to the ground,

but Cam wouldn't let him. He pushed him off and they rolled among the stones and the pine needles, clasped in each other's hateful hold, their legs tangled and attacking. A squirrel screamed above them from a tree. Birds took flight, winging away from the man-battle below. The combatants roared at each other, their voices echoing in the forest—and then Ty shoved Cam against a pile of sticks. Cam cried out as one jagged point scraped his flesh, and Ty took advantage of the moment, pinning the Ruler at last with his legs. He went for Cam's neck, his powerful hands curled around the throat; but Cam groped beneath him for the stick, and when he found it, he swung it out, point down, into the murderer's side. Ty howled, releasing him instantly as he threw himself to the ground, clasping his bloody wound.

Cam mastered him easily then. He stabbed the wild man with that jagged stick until every gasp of life had spurted out of him and every agonizing memory of his own had been avenged.

"I just can't understand it," said Atanelle.

Giles gazed at her. The three exiles from upstairs were waiting in the dining room. They had been there a long time, sitting around the table, each lost in silent thought, silent prayer that their friend would be saved. Atanelle's words came as an intrusion on that vigil and Paragrin frowned.

"What can't you understand?" asked Giles gently.

"This sudden heroism!" she exclaimed. "Why, Kerk's the most selfish person I know."

"Then you don't know him very well," snapped Paragrin from across the table. "He did *your* job, Atanelle, by saving Cam's life." Atanelle's eyes widened, and Paragrin scowled, scraping her nails impatiently against the chair. "We can only hope Cam's still alive. Who knows what that murderer could have done to him by now." She got to her feet. "I'm going to go look for him!"

"Jentessa told you to wait," said Giles, catching her hand. "And I think—"

All at once a figure passed behind them into the dining room. All three spun around, their hearts stopped in their chests.

"Oh, Grandfather!" said Paragrin, stamping her foot. "What are *you* doing here?"

"No need to get testy," Ram replied. "You should all be more easy by now, shouldn't you? I warned you in time about Magramid; everything's fine again." He edged past Paragrin and stopped where a bowl of nuts sat on the table.

"You weren't in the court this afternoon, were you?" said Atanelle.

"Glory, no. I kept as far apart from that mess as I could, and why not?" Ram stretched a bony arm across Giles to get at the nuts.

"Our friend Kerk is upstairs with a knife wound," explained Giles, watching as Ram took a walnut. "It could be fatal. The blade was meant for his brother, but Kerk took it himself."

Ram's mouth fell open. "No! Really?" He set the nut between his teeth. "What would he do a stupid thing like that for?"

Paragrin turned her head slowly to stare at her grandfather. "Get out of here," she said. "Take that nut from your mouth and leave before I—"

"But you don't understand," Ram protested, putting the wet shell back in the bowl. "I live here now."

Paragrin's eyes widened. She rose from her chair, her complexion turning a warning shade of red.

"This, after all I did for you!" Ram said, clenching his fists. "I risked my life telling you about Magramid. You should be hailing me as a hero!"

"Get out!"

Atanelle rose to help him leave, but she needn't have bothered. Paragrin seized the walnut and flung it after Ram, who moved quickly for his great years and disappeared.

The walnut bounced off the stairway and landed on the entrance-hall floor, where it rocked for a moment before lying still. Paragrin remained standing, her eyes fixed on the empty entrance, her fingers curling and uncurling on the back of the chair.

Giles watched her. "You have to let Cam do what he has to do," he said quietly. "You can't interfere. His brother's life must be avenged, or he must die in the attempt."

"That's not how we do things in this colony," said Paragrin sharply, turning on him. "Besides, you don't know Cam. He'd sooner die than harm another person."

"I'll go look for him," said Atanelle, getting to her feet. "I'll bring him back alive, or drag that savage back dead."

Paragrin glanced at Giles. "Bring them both alive if you can, Atanelle," she said softly, "so we can bring Ty to our more civilized justice."

* * *

Outside, it was growing dark. Aridda brought in fatlamps, illuminating Jentessa as she bent over Kerk. She had been that way for over an hour, watching, waiting. A bandage was wrapped tightly now between Kerk's ribs and waist, and even though he had not yet opened his eyes, the bleeding had stopped. Ellagette, with Boon fallen to an uneasy sleep in her arms, tried to take comfort from this, but Jentessa would say nothing. And now, as the glow flickered across her face, she saw the Half-Divine was just as grim as she had been before.

"When is it going to end?" Ellagette moaned at last. "When is he going to wake, or . . ."

"Soon," said Jentessa. "There is nothing more we can do for his wound."

"He isn't perspiring as much," offered Aridda. "He's warmer."

"His pulse is weak, his breathing uneven," said Jentessa. "He'll either die now or wake, and if he wakes, we can only hope he'll be strong enough to overcome the initial pain, because if he isn't—"

Suddenly Kerk took in a gasp, a sharp drag of breath that made everyone in the chamber jump. Ellagette set Boon down and raced to the bed, but Jentessa knocked her away.

"Stay back!" she commanded.

Kerk's eyes shot open, but they weren't focused, darting around the room as he fought against the pain. As Aridda went to hold back the frightened child, Kerk writhed on the bed, his bandage discoloring suddenly with new blood. Jentessa tried to quiet him with words, but it was when she

200

took his hands, when she wove her strong fingers between his, pushing, that Kerk turned his energy to her. Jentessa stared back at him, the intensity of their gaze echoed in their shuddering hands. Kerk's fingers curled around her palms, cutting into her skin, yet Jentessa paid it no mind. She closed her eyes in concentration; so did he. For a moment the room was charged with the energy between them. Ellagette had to bite her thumb to keep from crying out, and still the hands clenched around each other, shaking with the pressure.

And then Jentessa let him go. Ellagette's eyes widened with terror, but his arms didn't fall to the bed. Kerk groaned and uncurled his grip slowly, his hands returning to his sides. Jentessa's shoulders fell as she let out her breath, and when she gazed down again at Kerk, he looked up at her with the sharpness back in his eyes.

Ellagette squeezed Boon's hand in hers.

Kerk blinked at Jentessa, not fully understanding what had happened; but when he saw Ellagette beyond, a weak grin crept across his face.

Jentessa only warned Ellagette to be gentle when she came running up to kiss him. The Half-Divine wiped her face with her hand before Aridda offered her a cloth.

"Ho, there," Kerk mumbled as he reached out to Boon. The boy erupted into smiles.

"You're a hero!" he exclaimed, and Kerk raised a brow. "Really?"

Boon nodded. "We waited for you, Kerk," he said, and glanced up at Ellagette. "We both did."

Aridda watched Jentessa in silence, studying the Half-

Divine with open admiration. "That was a miracle there, wasn't it?" she said at length.

"He was lucky" was all Jentessa said.

"Of that," replied Aridda, "I have no doubt."

"Cam!"

Paragrin leapt from the chair as her mate limped into the entrance hall, but her joy faded when she saw his condition. His clothes were hanging from his body in shreds, his face and hands were disfigured with swelling, but even this was not the worst of it.

"You're covered with blood," said Paragrin. She went forward to touch him, but was uncertain where to do it. That he could even walk after so much bleeding was amazing. Atanelle came into the entrance hall behind him, strangely silent and grave.

Cam grinned. "It's not my blood!" he declared. "I killed him, Paragrin. A death for a death. Kerk's murder is avenged!"

She stared at him, not believing what she had heard. Then a footfall on the stairs made everyone turn. Jentessa paused on the step when she saw Cam.

"What's the news?" asked Paragrin, her voice trembling. Jentessa was looking so solemnly at Cam that she was certain it was bad.

Jentessa kept her eyes on Cam. "Your brother lives," she said.

Paragrin shrieked with happiness, and grabbed the hands of Giles, who danced with her.

A broad smile broke across Cam's swollen lips, a light bursting from inside as the unexpected tidings reached his heart. And then, suddenly, his face fell, his eyes turning all at once hollow with dread. He looked slowly from his bloody hands to Jentessa, who still watched him from the stairs.

"Oh, my Maker . . ." he gasped. "My Maker!" His voice lifted. "*Jentessa! What have you done to me?*"

26

Outside, as the night deepened, the House at the head of the court was lit about with fatlamps and torches. It was quiet within, except when the happy laughter of the boy rose from Kerk's chamber.

Atanelle, waiting on the landing between the two rooms, debated whether or not she should hush him, when the deer-pelt curtain behind her was drawn aside and Paragrin handed out to her the bloody clothes that Cam had worn.

"Burn them," said Paragrin. "They can't be salvaged, anyway."

Atanelle took the clothes. "Is he any——?" she asked.

Paragrin began a reply, but caught Jentessa watching her from the entrance hall. Her mouth closed, though her eyes lingered on the Half-Divine, and she turned back into the chamber without another word.

Atanelle sighed and, tucking the clothes under her arm, clumped heavily down the stairs. Jentessa moved off, not wanting any conversation, even if Atanelle could have thought of what to say; but Giles hurried out from the dining room when he saw her descend.

"Cam's still upset?" he asked.

"I suppose so," Atanelle replied. "I think he's sorry now for killing Ty when Kerk wasn't even dead."

Giles shrugged it off. "I don't see what else he could have done. His desire was perfectly natural. In my colony—"

"You really come from another colony?" Atanelle exclaimed, greatly impressed.

"Yes, I do," said Giles, brightening. "And we have a rather different way of living there, a better way, I think. Duty always takes precedent over personal wants." He pulled on his beard, smiling at her. "You can understand that, can't you? You could live in that sort of place and be quite at home, couldn't you?"

"Yes, I suppose I could," she said thoughtfully. "Duty has always been my life's calling."

"That's what I hoped you'd say!" Giles took her by the arm and pulled her from the entrance hall, outside, away from the Half-Divine's hearing. Light spilled down from the Rulers' chamber, illuminating them in the night.

"As dedicated as we are to our work," said Giles excitedly, "there is one duty neither one of us has yet performed."

Atanelle stared at him, clutching the bundle of clothes to her chest defensively. Something alarming was about to happen, she knew it.

"It is my particular duty as a ruler, and your general duty as a woman," said Giles, "to bring children into the world —or, in my case, to bring an heir." His eyes widened. "I want you to return with me to my colony and become my mate."

"Oh, my Maker . . ." she said.

"I know this is sudden," said Giles, "and I don't mean to

make it sound *just* practical, although it *is*, wonderfully so."
He stepped apart, his gnarly hands spread joyously before
him as an extension of his words. "I have never, never in
my long life met any woman who possessed your special
kind of beauty: the kind that lies in both physical and moral
strength." He gazed at her, his arms falling, weakened, to
his sides. "You have so much of both, Atanelle," he said.
"Will you be my mate?"

She stared at him still, her mouth fallen open in
astonishment.

His courage faltered. "Is there someone else?" he asked.
"Is that why you hesitate? Or is it my age? I know I'm past
my youth, but I *am* Ruler—that should make up for it in
your eyes. Think of it! You'll be Joined to a ruler." He held
out his recovered Amulet proudly.

Atanelle gazed back at him, but her heart clutched and
she looked away, flustered, wadding up the bloodied clothes
in her hands.

"There is another, isn't there?" asked Giles, dismayed.

"No," said Atanelle. "At least . . . not in the way you
mean."

A moment passed. Giles pulled on his beard. "Well? Will
you give me an answer, then?"

"I can't," she said, and glanced at him. "I—I have to think
about it, about leaving the Melde . . ."

"There's nothing for you here," said Giles. "No one ap-
preciates you."

"That's not true," said Atanelle. "There're my friends, my
Rulers Paragrin and Cam."

Giles shook his head. "Paragrin isn't half as dutiful as you
are—or I am. And Cam . . . that boy has troubles: good

instincts, but no strength to believe in them. He's weak, Atanelle."

"He's not!" she said, flushing. "You're just seeing him at a bad time. He was wonderfully strong before, strong in his convictions."

"Then he's changed, hasn't he?" said Giles. Seeing the hurt in her eyes, he added more gently, "Why are we arguing? Atanelle . . ." He held out a hand to her. "You're closer to my way of thinking than to his. Admit it. We could lead a good, honest life together in the Vasser."

Atanelle let him hold her hand, let him rub it gently. No one had ever touched her like that, and it made her shiver.

"Give me a day," she mumbled. "I just have to think things over."

"All right," said Giles reluctantly. "But no more than that. I have to get home to my work." He held her hand a moment more, then released it, excusing himself to go to his makeshift bed within the House.

Atanelle stayed outside, alone with her thoughts. Above, the light from the Rulers' chamber still fell upon her, and upon the bloodstained clothes in her arms.

"Cam *is* strong," she whispered, pressing the clothes to her bosom. "He hasn't really changed, has he . . ."

"Now, I won't tolerate this sort of defiance," declared Aridda, folding her arms beneath her bosom. "You're only a child, and you'll do as I say."

"I won't," said Boon. "You're not my mother! Kerk can tell me what to do." He swung around the bedpost and smiled at him.

Kerk laughed. "Oh, that's how it's going to be, is it? Well,

I'm too tired to make any decisions. You listen to what Ellagette says; you like her, don't you? She'll be your mother tonight."

"Well, all right." His mouth set, Boon turned toward her, waiting for the judgment.

"I think you should sleep, too," said Ellagette, smiling, "and apart from Kerk, as Aridda told you. You're too full of energy to stay with a hurt person; you'd keep him awake all night, and he needs his rest."

"I wouldn't," said Boon. "And I don't have to mind anyone!"

"Ho, there," said Kerk, pushing himself up on his elbows. "What kind of talk is this? Is this being responsible?"

Boon frowned. "Do I always have to be responsible?"

"After what I did today, you ask me that?" Kerk replied. "How are you going to grow up to be a hero like me if you don't start behaving now?"

Boon considered this.

"I'll tuck you in downstairs," said Ellagette, stifling a laugh. "Will that make it better?"

"I think you should quit the chamber, too, my friend," remarked Aridda. "He does need his rest."

Boon applauded.

"Well, all right," said Ellagette, "if I can stay a minute longer with him."

"Then so will I stay," Boon announced, but Aridda led him firmly away.

When they were alone at last, Ellagette slid her hand into Kerk's. "How are you doing?" she asked gently; "really doing?"

"Wonderfully," he said, "now that I've got you back again."

"That's me who should be saying that," said Ellagette. She gazed at him. "I thought I had lost you twice, Kerk."

"Not a chance of it," he said. For a moment they were silent together, each hand caressing the other. Then, as Kerk watched her intently, his voice took on a carefree air. "So!" he said. "How do you like my little friend Boon? A rascal, isn't he? But good beneath it all."

"He reminds me of someone," said Ellagette, "especially with that part about being *responsible* all the time. You've . . . taken him on?"

Kerk nodded. "He didn't have anyone else. He was a mess on his own, getting into trouble. He needs me to help guide him in life."

Ellagette smiled. "One blind man following another," she said.

"No, I'm serious! I've changed, Ellagette—at least a little bit. I really want to raise him, to take on that responsibility. I never knew how fine it could be, to have someone put their trust in me so completely."

"You never knew, because you never looked," said Ellagette quietly.

"I didn't mean that," Kerk said. "I was an idiot, I admit it!" He reached for her again. "But I've changed toward you as well. Paragrin will back me—I didn't sleep with anyone while I was gone. I was so good!"

Ellagette widened her eyes. "Such sacrifice!"

"It *was*; you know me."

"Too well," she said.

"I mean what I say, Ellagette, and I—I—" Kerk bit his lip. "I want to reconsider . . ."

"Reconsider what?"

"I want to reconsider what you said when we had that argument before I left."

Ellagette raised a brow. "You mean about Joining?"

"Yes. That's it. I want you to think about it now; especially now that I come with another burden . . ."

Color rose in Ellagette's cheek. "You're actually asking me? I can hardly believe it."

"Think of it!" Kerk exclaimed. "Me, you, and Boon! A ready-made family."

"I would want children of my own as well," warned Ellagette.

"Hundreds of them! We'll start making them now." Kerk lunged for her, but gave a cry of pain and sank back against his pillow. "Later," he said. "We'll start later." He grinned weakly. "But do you like the idea? Really like it? And do you like Boon?"

"He'll certainly need my lighter influence, what with all your tiresome talk of responsibility," said Ellagette, and smoothed back the curls around Kerk's temple, gazing at him. "Yes," she said more seriously. "I do like Boon. Very much."

Kerk grinned again and held out his arms. Ellagette leaned into them and kissed him.

"Quit that!" she squealed, as he tried unlacing her blouse. "You need your rest."

Kerk groaned. "If that knife didn't kill me, rest will," he said.

When Atanelle had stumbled home, Jentessa ventured outside, turning to look back at that window on the second floor: the Rulers' chamber, with the light shining down upon the grass. She could feel Cam's presence there; she could feel his pain—and his anger. She could feel a lot of anger.

Within that chamber, Paragrin was hard at work trying to erase Cam's madness. She had put a new nightdress on his body, its crisp, clean fabric hanging pure against his skin; she had tended to his wounds, bandaging three places; and now she sat beside him on the bed with a dish of salve, wiping the residues of blood from his forehead and chin.

Her ministrations completed, she sat back and studied her patient, only to find her work was for nothing; the eyes betrayed every injury she had tried so hard to cover.

"Everything I believed in has been refuted," said Cam.

"Not everything," she whispered.

"Everyone I trusted has deceived me," said Cam.

"Not everyone," said Paragrin. "Not me, not yourself."

"Not myself?" he cried, turning to her. "I'm the worst offender, the worst kind of hypocrite! Even Magramid was more honest in her evil—obvious to everyone except to me. Did I tell you that Notts warned me about her early on? Thanks to my stupidity, she stayed to murder him for his insight. Add one more death to my conscience!"

"You weren't responsible for his death," said Paragrin.

Cam gave a laugh and rose from the bed to pace. " 'Nothing is unforgivable, Notts,' I told him. My Maker, what a fool I was."

"You believe in the good of people," said Paragrin, "remember?"

"Well, Magramid wasn't 'people,' was she? Neither is Jentessa, who left me to—to be violated by that—that—"

His fists clenched, his body trembling as he remembered the horror.

"Don't think about that," said Paragrin, rising to put her arms around him. "Try to forget about what happened."

"I don't want to forget!" cried Cam, breaking from her hold. "I don't ever want to forget what happens when you put your faith in a Half-Divine, in the Maker Itself! If I forget, if I forgive, I'll do it again."

"Why do you blame Jentessa for what Magramid did?" demanded Paragrin.

Suddenly two knocks were heard outside the entrance to the chamber. The Rulers stared at each other, uncertain; then Paragrin went to the doorway and drew aside the curtain.

It was Aridda. "I'm sorry to interrupt," she said, "but your voices are echoing throughout the House. Your brother needs his rest," she said, turning to Cam, "and I would think you do, too. It's been quite a day."

Cam pushed his fingers through his hair. "Yes, it has," he said. "Thank you, Aridda. You're right about Kerk. We'll be quiet."

Aridda moved her gaze from one Ruler to the other, then nodded and went out. Cam let out a long breath and sank down on the bed, his stare fixed on the floorstones.

Paragrin watched him. "It was Jentessa who saved your brother's life, you know," she said.

Cam closed his eyes. "I know."

Paragrin sat down beside him, wanting to hold him but fighting the urge, trying to give him time to think. "When I was in the Vasser," she said quietly, "everything seemed upside down. No one looked beyond themselves to trust in the Maker; everyone hated their Half-Divine. Strange as it was, I could understand it there. But *here*," she took his hand gently in her own, pressing it, "here we have reason to believe in the greater good. I want to feel secure again. Jentessa can't be the villain you imagine her to be. Even if she came too late to save us from every hurt, at least she came. And she rid the earth of Magramid. It seems so clear to me who's the villain and who's the hero. Can't you see that?" She looked at him hopefully, but his hand remained impassive in hers, his eyes intent on the floorstones.

"This colony feels upside down to me," he said. "Through no fault of ours, through no choice of mine, it's been turned into the Vasser, and Giles and I behave no differently now."

"Giles would chop a man's hand off for stealing and call it justice!" said Paragrin.

"And for the injury of my brother, I killed a man. *I killed a man.*" Cam shook his head. "I'm no more civilized."

"But you don't call it justice," said Paragrin, "and that's the difference."

He looked up at her, his hand returning her pressure at last. "I wish I could believe you," he said, "but I'm not that gullible anymore."

Outside, Jentessa turned from the window, discouraged. They were so young! So very young in their knowledge of the world—and of themselves.

There was still one more matter for her attention. That much was obvious.

27

There had to be a celebration dinner the next day. Paragrin saw no way around it. After all, despite the tragedies, there *were* reasons to celebrate: she and Kerk had come home; Kerk had risked his life and recovered; Giles was the first foreign ruler to visit the Melde; and, of course, Magramid had been exiled from the earth. That last accomplishment had gone rather unsung after Kerk's heroics and Cam's "alteration," but Paragrin was determined to acknowledge it, despite her mate's objections.

"You should be the first to celebrate her banishment," she told him. "At least she can't descend on people anymore in human guise."

"I am grateful," said Cam, "but since Jentessa allowed her to come here in the first place, I'd be doubly grateful if she had followed her sister to the sky."

There was no arguing with him. It was enough, thought Paragrin, that he had agreed to sit at the same table with Jentessa; a jolly reconciliation between them was too much to hope for. So Paragrin was left to arrange the festivities with less than festive anticipation, armed with nothing else but the conviction that at least an appearance of harmony ought to be presented.

After Aridda had spent all day working in the kitchen, the appointed time at last arrived. Kerk hobbled down from his sick bed in glory, supported by his admiring train of Ellagette and Boon; Giles came to the table, all impatience, drumming his gnarly fingers against the wood; and Jentessa came into the House next, accompanied by two very unlikely-looking escorts.

"These men are from the potter's shop," explained Jentessa as Paragrin eyed the guests suspiciously. "Due to the earthquakes, their shop is temporarily out of commission, so I offered these workers some employment as servers at our feast."

"Here?" said Paragrin. "Tonight?" She drew Jentessa out of their hearing. "Don't you think they're a little . . . rough . . . to trust with everything this evening?" she asked. "You know the mood is somewhat delicate. I'm afraid that—"

Jentessa held up her hand. "Trust me," she said. "These men are quite reliable. I chose them specifically for that reason."

"Oh," said Paragrin. "Well . . ."

"And think how pleased Aridda will be to have a little help," said Jentessa. She smiled and motioned the two men out to the kitchen, then settled at her place between Paragrin and Giles.

The last two chairs remained empty for several awkward minutes. The potters were already marching out to fill the goblets with wine, when Cam came downstairs. It was obvious he had not made the slightest effort to dress for the festivities, and Paragrin was about to chide him for it—

gently—when she saw his already tight expression stiffen. She traced his stare to the servers.

Cam pulled her aside. "Why are those men here?" he demanded.

"To help Aridda."

"Do you know the sort of men they are?" he demanded again. "They're followers of Fratt."

"Of whom?"

"The blacksmith! That idiot who challenged me in the open court."

"The blacksmith challenged you in the open court?" exclaimed Paragrin, her eyes widening.

"Oh. That's right," said Cam, meeting her stare, "you weren't here. Well, it was nothing. The idiot kept calling me a 'posy,' and I had to go out to confront him. It was ridiculous. I'm surprised Atanelle didn't tell you about it."

"There's hardly been time for a chat," said Paragrin. "What happened? Was there a fight?"

"No! Of course not. Well, he hit me, *and* hit me, but I didn't fight back, not once." Cam broke into a smile. "You should have seen the way I faced him down, Paragrin," he said. "The people went wild with cheers for me. I'd never felt so strong in all my—"

Caught with this smile upon him, Cam met Jentessa's eye. He recovered himself quickly and looked away.

"Who brought these ruffians into the House?" he demanded.

"Jentessa."

He flushed. "I want them out. Now."

"No! Cam . . ." She pulled him farther from the table.

"Let's not have more confrontations tonight, please! They're all right. Jentessa wouldn't have brought them here if they weren't."

Cam scowled. "It's not enough that our outside lives have to be controlled by a Half-Divine," he muttered; "now she's choosing our servants. I don't know why I wear a ruler's iron at all."

He was angry with her and Jentessa both now, Paragrin knew; but he let the potters stay, moving brusquely past them to take his chair at the far end of the table. After acknowledging Boon on his left, he leaned across the empty place at his right to talk to Giles.

"Is this the way it is at the Vasser?" he whispered. "A Ruler never having any real sense of control?"

"What control he has, he must wrench from the immortals," said Giles, and downed his goblet of wine in one gulp. "Where is Atanelle?" he said, turning in his chair to peer out into the entrance hall.

Cam wound his fingers around the goblet stem and, after a moment of consideration, downed his own wine. "I'll have more," he told the potter who was bringing out the plates. "That is, if I'm qualified to make one decision by myself." He glared at Jentessa, but she wasn't looking at him.

The three Rulers sat in silence then, while rolls were set out upon the table and fresh wine poured. The curly-haired potter honored with this last duty partook of the wine himself when he didn't think anyone was watching. Paragrin saw him do it—more than once—and almost said something to Jentessa, but decided at the last moment to hold her tongue. No confrontations tonight. She turned to talk to Ellagette instead, but the three occupants of that side of the table were so engrossed in their own cheerful chatter that she hadn't the heart to disturb them. Paragrin rested her chin in her hand and watched the love sparkle from Ellagette's eyes to Kerk's, and found it on the whole wonderfully depressing.

Cam emptied his second goblet, but Giles only clenched his in his fist, his weathered face hardening all the more with frustration.

The curly-haired server ambled out from the kitchen. "The cook says she has to serve the venison now, even if all of you aren't here," he announced.

"Who's missing?" asked Kerk, rising out of his confidential talk with Boon and Ellagette.

"Atanelle, rot you," Giles returned.

"Oh," said Kerk. "Was she invited?"

He was spared any further remonstrance by the timely arrival of the warrior. Atanelle stood in the portal, very unsure of herself, and looked timidly at the stares she was receiving.

Kerk was the first to find his voice. "What did you do to your hair?" he exclaimed.

"You've undone your braid!" said Paragrin, rising quickly from her chair. "It looks lovely, Atanelle."

"I was hoping no one would notice," she said, pushing the tresses back behind her broad shoulders. She glanced about to find her chair, and almost left when she saw the two men she'd be sitting next to. Paragrin captured her in time, though, and brought her in between Cam and Giles, seating her firmly in the chair.

"Not notice?" Kerk said, unable to control his astonishment at her transformation. "Why, you haven't untied that braid of yours since I've known you, Atanelle. You have no idea, Giles"—he grinned across the table—"that you're seeing an entirely new woman!"

Giles laughed with relief. "I suspect there's a whole side to our friend that none of you has seen," he said gaily, and reached for her hand beneath the table.

Atanelle moved it quickly to take her goblet and would not meet his eyes. She had never felt so embarrassed.

"Well!" said Paragrin, planting herself back in her chair. "Now that we're all finally assembled, let's begin our celebration."

Boon clapped his hands in anticipation, and the potters moved determinedly—if unsteadily—to bring in the roast.

All in all, it was disappointing fare for a special dinner. Try as they might to convince themselves otherwise, Aridda was only an indifferent cook. More than one guest in lowered tones allowed as how the feast would have been improved if Cam had been the chef. Cam agreed—in louder tones—and encouraged everyone to drown the taste with wine. Paragrin, fuming at the opposite end of the table, would have been hard put to decide which man was becoming more inebriated, her mate or the curly-haired potter; but since no one else seemed to be bothered by their behavior, she pretended not to notice. Kerk, Ellagette, and Boon were still engrossed in their private conversation, Jentessa seemed perfectly oblivious to everything, and Giles wouldn't stop talking to Atanelle. Atanelle . . . Well, thought

Paragrin as she watched her, at least she wasn't the only one having a miserable time.

Atanelle, her appetite lost long before, sat in silence between the two men. Although Giles's chatter was considerably less confident than it had been at the start of the meal, it was nevertheless continuing. She wasn't listening to a word he said; her eyes were cast down, only occasionally lifting to steal a glance at her Ruler.

Sweet Maker, thought Atanelle, watching how Cam, loosened with too much drink, was fumbling with his meat knife, he *has* changed . . . His eyes were red, his laughter too free and loud, his manner insulting.

"It's disgraceful," said Giles, leaning closer to her ear. "This sort of drunkenness is sickening in anyone, let alone a leader."

She looked away as the servers reached to clear the plates.

"Atanelle! You've hardly eaten a thing!" said Cam, suddenly noticing as her food passed before him. "That isn't like you at all. You usually pack in more than I do."

Atanelle blushed, a deep, awful blush that made her face burn. She stared intently down at the floor as Cam found someone else to talk to.

"This is intolerable," growled Giles. "I won't allow him to—"

"No," said Atanelle, staying Giles beneath the table. "Don't."

Giles paused, then reached under to take her hand. "You deserve better than what this colony can offer you," he whispered.

This time Atanelle didn't pull away. She hated Cam more than she had ever hated anyone.

"Well!" said Paragrin, eager to conclude the joyous occasion, "I think it's time to end our feast with a few tributes. I would suggest that everyone fill their goblets, but it seems some of us have already drained the grape . . ."

The curly-haired server, standing off with his companion, gave a raucous laugh, and his companion hit him.

"Don't do that," said the curly-haired server.

Paragrin ground her teeth until he had finished speaking. "So—why don't we just raise our goblets," she said, "and give thanks first to our brave friend Kerk—not only for his sacrifice yesterday on the court, but also for the good progress of his recovery."

Boon cheered the loudest as Kerk pushed himself up from his chair. "Thank you all," he said. "It's a marvelous feeling, being a hero—almost as wonderful as becoming the father-mate in what will soon be a family." More applause then from Boon. "But to be honest," Kerk continued, "to be truly responsible in my heart, I must share the title of hero with our protectress"—he bowed to Jentessa—"who not only rid the earth of Magramid but also saved my life! And also I must share the title with my big brother Cam, who showed uncommon bravery by killing the man who tried to kill me! I am impressed. Once again, Giles, you see before you a new person. Cam would never have touched him before."

"Yes! Let's all pay tribute to Cam and Jentessa," Cam exclaimed, getting to his feet. "And Magramid, too, while we're at it. The three murderers! Of course, Jentessa's influence was less direct with old Notts, but it all boils down to the same thing, doesn't it?"

Paragrin confronted him across the table, determined to conclude. "And to Giles," she said, her eyes fixed threateningly on her mate, "who is the first foreign ruler to visit our colony. Let's celebrate his coming—and his role in rescuing the Melde."

Cam glared back at her, his mouth quivering with some yet unformed retort, when Giles pushed up from his chair.

"There is more than that to celebrate tonight," he declared, his beard thrust out triumphantly. "Although I haven't yet received her final word, I believe I can now safely proclaim that—"

Suddenly a loud crash sounded behind them. The curly-haired potter had dropped the last jug of wine, smashing it on the floor. "Oh, no . . ." he sighed, but his companion, having just been drenched by the wine, gave a more physical reaction: he shoved his friend against the wall. His lamentation for the lost wine forgotten, the curly-haired server swung out his fist, and a terrible brawl began.

Paragrin groaned. Was there no end to the evening's disasters?

"No, no, Atanelle," said Cam, pushing her down as she tried to get up from her seat to subdue them. "I'll take care of it . . ."

"You're in no shape to do anything!" barked Giles, greatly annoyed by the interruption of his announcement. "I'll rule this colony as a colony ought to be ruled."

But Cam, coloring slightly from this sting, was not to be put off. Both men went toward the curly-haired server, who had cornered his assailant and was now pummeling him soundly.

"Jentessa," wailed Paragrin, but the Half-Divine didn't seem in the least surprised by any of this. She merely turned in her chair to watch, wiping her mouth delicately with her napkin.

"You stop this!" demanded Giles, reaching for the server. He pulled him back, but the potter, inspired by the success of the fight, only shrugged him off and went in to punch his companion some more.

Giles was not one to take such defiance lightly. With a roar, he threw out his arms, spun the man around—and fell back against the table, having been struck across the jaw.

For a moment—after the gasps—no one said anything. The curly-haired server was too confused by what had just happened, his companion too battered, and Giles himself was so stunned by this personal attack that he could not believe it had occurred. But in the following seconds, as the pain in his jaw began to flare, his eyes rounded with rage and he seized a meat knife from the table.

"Giles!" cried Paragrin as the Vasser Ruler started for the potter.

It took Cam a moment longer than it would have ordinarily to react. But when he realized the next instant what Giles was about to do, he threw himself between the men.

"Get out of my way!" yelled Giles. "It's the law: Death to the man who strikes a ruler."

"It's not *our* law," Cam shouted, and struggled to pull the knife from his hand. A moment longer and his youthful

223

strength won over—the weapon dropped to the floor, and Cam kicked it out of reach and stood back, his eyes wide upon the other.

"You coward," said Giles, as the servingmen escaped into the kitchen. "You had no right to prevent good justice."

"It's not considered justice here," said Cam. "No one should die for striking a ruler, for striking anyone. We'll handle his punishment in our own way, Giles."

"Your ways are soft . . . Shameful! Aren't they, Atanelle?" declared Giles, turning to look at his ally. His sureness froze upon his face: Atanelle wasn't watching him. She was watching—no—gazing at Cam, her first smile of the night broken across her face.

"Fight me, rot you!" cried Giles, spinning back in despair to his rival. "I'll prove who's more the man."

Cam let his arms fall to his sides. He looked back at Giles and shook his head. "No, I won't fight you. Giles," he said more gently, "I haven't been at my best, either. Let's just forget about our—"

Giles threw out his fist in one last attempt to win Atanelle. Caught unprepared, Cam was knocked to the floor, and everyone at the table rose in horror—everyone except Jentessa, who continued, simply, to observe.

Giles readied himself for defense while Cam, impeded by both pain and wine, took some time to struggle to his feet. But when he faced Giles again, he didn't—even then— raise his fists.

Giles stared at him. "I do not understand your ways," he said. Behind him, Atanelle moved and, without a word, stood beside her Ruler, her eyes lowered.

Giles saw it all then. "*Or yours!*" he said, and removed himself from the room.

A moment passed. Cam let out his breath, then found his legs beginning to buckle beneath him. He leaned on his chair as Paragrin hurried to his side.

"Are you all right?" she asked, helping him sink into his seat.

"I've just had too much to drink," said Cam, and shook his head, stroking Paragrin's arm. "I'm sorry I got myself drunk," he muttered.

Paragrin knelt down beside him. "You're trembling," she said, reaching for his hand.

"Am I?" Cam laughed, then looked at her, a faint smile lingering on his face. "I think I'm going to be all right, Paragrin," he said.

She gazed back, then wrapped her arms around him.

Boon was disgusted by this display, though Kerk grinned to see it, and Ellagette slipped her hand quietly into his.

Jentessa rose and moved out into the entrance hall, where Atanelle had gone to sit by herself upon the steps.

"You could go to him still," said Jentessa gently. "He can't sail his boat until sunrise."

Atanelle looked up at her, surprised, and then *not* surprised, that she seemed to know the situation.

"No," said Atanelle, wiping a tear bravely from her eye and rising. "You can't pretend something you don't feel, can you? Even if you wished you could."

"There may be others," said Jentessa.

Atanelle shrugged. "Doesn't matter." She gathered her hair behind her with a sigh and began, expertly, to braid it again. "I couldn't have been what he wanted me to be, anyway. You are who you are and you do what you do, right? Sooner or later, you have to accept that."

"Yes," said Jentessa, looking back at Cam as Paragrin wound him in her arms. "Sooner or later."

28

Giles left as the first light of day showed him home. Paragrin had been there to see him off; even Cam had come to express his own hopes that the two colonies could learn to accept each other's ways. Giles was doubtful, but without Atanelle there to confuse his priorities, he grudgingly agreed that there was no sense in fighting. An invitation was given—a tentative one—for Cam to visit the Vasser, and Paragrin hoped that Hanna would one day visit them.

"Tell her she can bring Meridor—if she wants to," said Paragrin, and Giles laughed. He let out his sail and, with an uncommonly good wind propelling him, floated away downriver, toward the sea.

"So," said Jentessa, who had come up quietly behind them, "the visitation between colonies has begun!" She shook her head. "The world will seem smaller now."

"Bigger, I should think," said Paragrin, turning to her, "with new places to explore."

"But less mystery," replied Jentessa. "Once, you thought the Melde's dominion stretched all around the earth."

"Now we know the truth," said Cam, leveling a look at her.

"Yes," said Jentessa. "And with every truth learned, a little dreaming is lost. Well, that's the way it's supposed to be. That's part of evolution, part of growing up."

She returned his look then, every bit as much independent defiance shining in her eyes as Cam held in his.

He gave a rueful smile. "Was that platitude for me?" he asked.

Jentessa looked away. "The irony," she said, gazing off across the river, "is that no matter how much we 'immortals'—to borrow Giles's term—try to manipulate you humans, we can never be completely sure what will happen. You *do* have a choice in the matter. Always."

"I doubt that," said Cam. "This is the first time in days that I've felt at all in control of my actions."

"Well, there's been more than our influence controlling you, then," replied Jentessa. "There's been a little human passion to account for, hasn't there, what with one thing or another . . . *We* can't be held responsible for your emotional reactions."

"It sounds as if you're not accepting responsibility for anything!" Cam said, coloring.

"Nonsense. We accept responsibility for the colonies' overall good, and for our own emotional reactions. We *do* have them, you know," said Jentessa, looking back at them; "or did you imagine we were perfect? Another dream dissolved . . .

"If I had been perfect," Jentessa continued, "I wouldn't have let my hatred of my sister get the better of me. I might have found a more—humane—way of baiting her. My apologies, Cam," she said, bowing, "but sometimes even the most cautious of souls is driven by desperation."

Cam glanced at her, then lowered his eyes. "Sometimes," he said quietly.

"Well! Enough of this lighthearted chatter," said Jentessa after a moment had passed. "Apparently I have work to do. It is the Maker's wish that I oversee the welfare of the Vasser, too, now that it's without a Half-Divine."

Paragrin laughed. "You have to take on the Vasser?" she exclaimed. "You have quite a job ahead of you!"

"If our friend Giles is any example of their deep-felt attitudes," said Jentessa.

"Which he is," put in Paragrin.

"Then I shouldn't waste another minute." Jentessa gazed at the Rulers. "You won't see me again," she said.

"But you'll be seeing us?" asked Paragrin.

"You may rely on it." Jentessa gave her a quick hug and stepped back, preparing to fade.

"Jentessa—" Cam began, suddenly looking up at her. She lifted her head.

He began a thought, then shut his mouth again, smiling.

". . . Understood," said Jentessa. "And take care." Closing her eyes, she shimmered softly and faded out of sight.

Cam reached for Paragrin's hand, squeezing it.

"You haven't a prayer," Atanelle shouted, hurrying out from the court to where the two Rulers stood on the riverbank. She was followed, hotly, by Ram, who was much out of breath from the race.

"Let me warn you," said Atanelle quickly, "he's about to ask you to let him stay in the Great House. I told him his time had run out, that you, my Ruler," she said, nodding to Paragrin, "had returned and now he would have to go. That was the agreement, wasn't it?"

"It was," said Cam.

"But that second room upstairs will go to waste after Kerk leaves," Ram panted. "I see no reason why I—a former leader of this fine colony, not to mention a hero in these latest adventures—shouldn't be allowed to stay in the Rulers' House!"

Atanelle narrowed her eyes. "I think it has something to do with your reprehensible past," she said.

"Now, Atanelle, I'm surprised at you," said Paragrin, putting an arm loosely around her shoulder. "You know our motto here: Nothing is unforgivable. Right, Cam?"

"Well," said Cam.

"How can I refuse my grandfather his rightful place?"

"Well, really," said Atanelle, staring at Paragrin in surprise.

Ram danced on the grass. "I always knew there was good family blood coursing through your veins!" he exclaimed. "We share true nobility, brilliance, and now the House as well."

"But not a floor," said Paragrin. "You can stay in the House, but not in that chamber upstairs. You can stay where you are—in that room off the kitchen."

"That stubby little closet!" Ram squawked.

"If," said Paragrin, "you agree to help Aridda whenever she needs you, washing the linens, cooking the food . . ."

"Gross indignities," Ram gasped; then: "All right. But don't blame me if you choke on a bone accidently left floating in the soup." He turned and stamped back into the court.

"Well," said Atanelle, watching him go, "the food can't taste any worse than it already does."

"Atanelle," said Cam, reaching for her braid, "you changed your hair back again."

She shrugged. "I was just being silly before," she said. "I don't know what I was thinking."

"It looked beautiful down," said Cam, running his fingertips along the weave, "but I like it better this way. It's more you, somehow."

"That's what I decided," she said.

Cam slipped his arm around her waist. "I'll have you know, Paragrin," he said, turning to his mate, "that all the while you were gone this woman never once faltered in her duty. She stayed by me every step of the way—even when I wasn't easy to be with."

"I don't doubt it for a minute," said Paragrin, and Atanelle blushed.

"I just want you to know how much I appreciate all that you've done, Atanelle," said Cam. "I don't know if I could have survived without you." He leaned across and kissed her on the cheek, which bloomed to an even deeper shade of pink beneath his touch.

"You couldn't have," she said softly, and excused herself, strolling off to attend to other matters of the Melde.

Paragrin laughed. "Oh, it's so good to have everything normal again!" she exclaimed. Cam took her hand and walked with her along the riverbank.

"There have been some changes, you know," he said, when they had gone a while in silence beside the water.

"I know," said Paragrin, "but natural ones . . . maybe?"

"I guess so." Cam stopped and turned to gaze at her. He put out a hand, gently, to her face, then leaned down to meet her lips. Paragrin reached up to him, folding her arms around his neck.

"I don't want to leave you ever again," she whispered. "I've come home! I'm ready now to stay."

"How I've missed you," said Cam, and caught her up in his strong arms, laughing.